THE PARADE

The Parade

M E GOLESWORTHY

Sospiro Publishing

The right of M E Golesworthy to be identified as author of this Work has been asserted by her in accordance with sections 77 and 78 of the Copyright, Designs and Patents Act 1988.

All rights reserved. No part of this publication may be reproduced, stored in retrieval system, copied in any form or by any means, electronic, mechanical, photocopying, recording or otherwise transmitted without written permission from the publisher. You must not circulate this book in any format.

ISBN: 978-1-8381343-6-5

This book is a work of fiction. Names, characters, places and incidents are either a product of the author's imagination or are used fictitiously.

A CIP catalogue record for this book is available from the British Library

Also by M E Golesworthy:
Intervention
The Waiter's Game
Tea and Moles in Brackenden Green

~ 1 ~

**Andalucía, Spain
February 2003**

'It's not a side of Spain they show tourists, is it?' Mapi closed the door and stepped out onto the cobbled street.

The photographer taking pictures of her mamá's house lowered his camera, looking guilty and putting the lens cap back on. 'No. No, it isn't. I'm sorry. I won't use these pictures unless you give the go ahead.'

A soft breeze blew gently between the whitewashed houses of the village and from the square at the end of the street came the tweeting of breakfasting sparrows.

'It wasn't here when we left yesterday afternoon,' he continued when she didn't respond, looking around the empty street. 'Do you know who's done it?'

Mapi joined the photographer and Peter, the producer, on the other side of the street. To the left of the front door, underneath the window bars, was the word *Rojo* written with red spray paint and a rather crude fascist flag. Whoever was responsible wasn't an artist. But then again, she guessed that wasn't the point.

'I don't know who, but I know why. It's because I'm here, and I won't live by their rules. I feel sorry for mamá, though. It's her home, and she will still be here when I return to Madrid.'

'Is she coming with us today?' Peter asked, hopeful.

Mapi shook her head. 'No. She's not feeling very well.' How could she explain to these men that the punishment inflicted on those who supported the losing side of the Spanish Civil War was so severe her mamá wouldn't talk about it? Isabel had begged her daughter not to get involved, even though they might find the one thing for which she'd been looking her whole life.

Peter smiled encouragingly. 'Perhaps she will feel better tomorrow.'

'Maybe,' Mapi answered absentmindedly before tearing her gaze away from the bright graffiti. She should stay and clean it up before her mamá saw it, but she had a feeling Isabel would not leave the house until the documentary crew had flown back to London. The neighbours, however, would see; they probably had already. Mapi wondered what would happen if someone knocked on the door and told mamá about it before she had a chance to remove the slur. But this was such an important day, and she had to go with the film crew because she might not get another chance such as this to tell the world, to remind the Spanish, about their history. She looked up at the producer, having made her decision. 'Come on. Let's see what they've found.'

From behind the threadbare curtains Isabel watched them leave, feeling nothing good would come of their project. After they disappeared, she stood still for several minutes, frozen in the same spot, and wondered how much of her daughter's fighting spirit had come from her family genes.

I am old now, papá. Much older than you ever had the chance to be. And I'm tired.

Well-known tears slipped down her cheeks, the way they always did when she spoke to him. Even after all these years she still found his loss difficult.

Stop it, Isabel. You are making a fool of yourself.

Leaning heavily on her cane she walked across the tiled floor of the front lounge and into her bedroom. It was sparsely furnished, with whitewashed walls and a crucifix hanging over the wooden double bed. A white plastic frame holding a picture of her husband sat on the chest of drawers, which she'd received for Christmas one year.

Slowly, she sat down on the bed and opened the drawer in her bedside table. It contained all her memories, both before and after the parade—the darkest year of her life. It formed a clear division in her life, one of innocence and hardship.

Amongst her possessions, the most treasured was an old photograph of her father. It was the only one she had and was likely the only one of him ever taken. His dark hair curled around the cap he had worn as he set off for the fields before the sun had risen over the mountains. Even now she could see his smile when he returned home and found her waiting for him at the crossroads.

~ 2 ~

Andalucía, Spain
April 1931 – October 1936

'You should be at home helping your mamá with the housework, Isabel. She will be cross with you.' His voice was tired, but a cheeky smile played on his lips as he lifted her up.

'I have worked all day, papá, and I wanted to meet you. Anyway, she's very happy because I gathered a whole basketful of wild asparagus this morning.'

He nodded and put her back down. Before she turned eight, he used to carry her all the way back home, but she guessed she was too old for that now.

'Are we having some for dinner tonight? That's good. Will you be cooking?'

Isabel hesitated before answering because she knew her mamá didn't want her cooking with hot oil; her friend's daughter had a pan of hot oil accidentally spilt over her legs. 'I will cook it for you, papá—with garlic. Just the way we like it.'

The sun threw its last rays over the pine-covered mountains surrounding them, and the world prepared for the stillness of another Andalucían evening. Cicadas buzzed in the background, and from the village down below came the ringing of church bells.

They walked along the hard-mud road, her little hand in his large one, and Isabel chatted about everything that had happened since he'd left the house that morning: the bread they had baked with acorn flour because they didn't have enough wheat, the wild asparagus she'd found, the antics of her little brother. He was only two years old and followed her everywhere on his stubbly little legs. He was her main responsibility, but apart from making sure he stayed within view of the house he wasn't any trouble. She knew her parents had been very happy when he was born; they finally had a son to leave the farm to, and to look after them in their old age. She had been quite jealous of Luis when he first arrived, but she was older now and it was nice to have someone to play with between helping her mamá around the house.

They had just passed the broken old gate to their neighbour's house when they heard the teenaged son, Antonio Chavez, call out. 'Señor Mosca. Have you heard the news?'

'No, I've just come back from the field.'

'The king has abdicated. Left the country too, I think.'

Papá walked back down the path to where Antonio now stood at the gate.

'Are you sure?'

'Yes, they announced it on the radio. This is turning out to be a good year: first the Republicans win the election, and now the king has left.'

Her father slowly nodded. 'Maybe everything will change now.'

Isabel pulled his sleeve to get his attention. 'We should go home now. Mamá will be waiting for us.'

'Hello, Isabel,' said Antonio. 'My little sister is back, and she's asked about you. You must come and visit her one day.'

Isabel knew that his sister, Pilar, had returned home after a prolonged visit with her cousins in Granada, but she didn't much like her. Pilar was three years older than Isabel, and even though she knew she had to be nice because Pilar's mamá had died the previous year, she didn't want to spend time with her. Not if she didn't have to. She decided the best way to get her papá back home was to ignore Antonio, so she did. Silence settled for a moment until she felt her papá grab her arm and shake it.

'Don't embarrass me, Isabel. Answer him.'

'I'm sorry, Señor, but I find your sister too bossy.'

For a moment her papá's grip hardened and she thought she might cry, but luckily Antonio started to laugh.

'You're right, she is bossy, but I think you two could be a match.' He turned his attention back to José, who had let go of his daughter's arm. 'Come and have a celebratory drink with my father.'

After a moment's hesitation he agreed and sent Isabel home to tell her mamá the news.

Glum, Isabel walked home alone, kicking stones as she went. She found her mamá in the kitchen scrubbing carrots, her dark hair tied into her usual tight bun at the back of her neck. When she heard the news, she shouted 'yes!' and ordered Isabel to look after her brother before throwing off her apron and running up the hill.

Isabel watched her disappear and then, with a disappointed sigh, she turned to find Luis.

It was late by the time her father returned home, and Isabel was asleep. When she woke she noticed the asparagus had gone, and it gave her some pleasure to think that papá was in the field, eating her asparagus for lunch

During the years before war tore their country apart, and brother turned on brother, the Mosca's were so sheltered on their little farm—La Quida—that unless a neighbour brought news they just continued on in the way they always had. In cities and towns across the country, churches were being burnt and strikers were murdered by the police. It was a time when political persuasions stood for more than just the party or organisation to which you belonged, it was your whole being: every cell in your body and every part of your soul.

Both of Isabel's parents had a spring in their step for the first few months that followed the election. Life's hardships seemed easier to bear now that a democratically elected left-wing government was in power. They believed things were going to change for the better. Now, there would be land for all to grow their food and nobody would go hungry. The unemployed dayworkers who drifted through the countryside with nowhere to live and nothing to eat would be looked after, their families no longer dying of starvation. Everybody would work for the benefit of their village or town, and the power would be shared evenly amongst those who worked the land.

Isabel, however, didn't notice anything different. Her father still worked from sunrise to sunset and attended union meetings, usually held at a neighbour's house now the meeting room in the village had been burnt down.

What upset Isabel most was that she now had to walk into the village to attend the new school. Her parents had argued about it, but papá had been adamant: his children would learn how to read and write so they didn't have to trust other people to read documents and papers for them. Her mamá had been against it, but after a long and drawn-out argument she'd given in.

'But I don't want to go.' Isabel cried as her mamá stood sternly, arms crossed, by the front door.

'Oh, you will go, and you will learn, and you'd better not cause this much fuss again. I have quite enough to do without you adding to it.'

When she didn't respond, her mamá took a step towards her and Isabel quickly decided it was best to run. Yet the shoes they now made her wear hurt her feet, and as soon as she was out of sight, she removed them.

The late-summer sun was already up, and its golden light flittered through the branches of the pine trees lining the well-trodden path from their house. The sound of a woodpecker searching for breakfast in a nearby tree accompanied the usual and constant buzz of cicadas.

With one shoe in each hand, Isabel wandered glumly down the path towards the crossroads. When she returned from school her chores would still be waiting for her; there wouldn't be time for anything else. Her parents didn't know how to read or write, so why did she have to learn? She'd have no need for it.

'Hola, Isabel.' Pilar called out while hanging up the washing. 'Are you going to school?' She wore one of her late mamá's dresses that was too big for her, and her thick black hair hung in a heavy plait down her back.

'Yes,' Isabel answered sullenly.

Pilar hung up the last shirt. 'You're lucky. I need to look after things here, so I can't go. Besides, I'm thirteen and too old to start school.'

'You're the lucky one. I wish I didn't have to go.'

Pilar laughed. 'You can look after this house and I'll go to school. I'd rather sit in a nice clean room learning things than looking after my father and brother.'

'Are you glad to be back?' Isabel asked to be polite, now feeling sorry for Pilar. She wished she, too, could come to school as she obviously wanted.

'Yes. It was nice to spend time with my aunts, but it's good to be home. There is no place like these mountains, and I missed my father and brother.'

'If you like, I can teach you what I learn in school.'

Pilar smiled. 'That would be very kind, Isabel.'

The faint sound of church bells sounded from the village and Isabel looked up in alarm. 'Oh no, I'm going to be late.'

'You'd better run,' Pilar said and shooed her away. 'Be good.'

Isabel ran down the hillside, already regretting her offer to Pilar. How would she find the time?

The new school had been built on the outskirts of the village, and most mornings Isabel could be seen running down the main street. The only time she could help Pilar learn to read and to write was in the morning before school. They would spend an hour at Pilar's kitchen table before Isabel heard the bells and bolted out the door.

Every time she was late her teacher, Señor Sanchez, slapped her hands with a stick he kept especially for that purpose. Her mamá found out and told Señor Sanchez why Isabel was late most mornings, but it made no difference. By that time Isabel wanted to go to school; not for herself but for Pilar, who absorbed everything Isabel told her. If Pilar had gone to school, Isabel thought, she would have ended up being a teacher.

Yet her schooling didn't last long. After Isabel's first year her parents decided she was needed at home to look after Luis. She should have been glad, but on market days in the village, when she saw her old school friends, she felt smaller than she used to.

To avoid them, Isabel would sometimes go to the local bar her Aunt Manda and Uncle Nicolas ran to play with her cousins for a little while. There would always be some snacks left over from lunch, and her aunt would let her take some home to her brother. As her mother and aunt argued from time to time, not speaking for months, Manda would often say, 'These are for Luis, not your mother.' Isabel, who liked her aunt, would dearly promise to make sure her mother didn't get a crumb.

After being swung on the swings by her older cousins at the back of the bar, or being taught how to catch lizards, she would walk back home and start her chores. Luis liked his treats as much as he liked the secrecy with which he received them; their mamá knew but pretended she didn't. Then, suddenly, the two sisters would be best friends again and snacks would be sent over to the whole family.

Life continued, but the changes her parents—and most of the village—had been sure would come with the new government never arrived. They had promised many things but when nothing happened the atmosphere at La Quida, and in the village, went back to the way it always had been. There would be no bright sunrise bringing equality to Spain, only more gunpowder added to the keg they were already sat on.

***

'You know you have to guess which hand,' Señor Chavez, Pilar's burly father, said. His voice was deep and always sounded as though he needed to clear his throat.

'That one.' Isabel pointed towards his right. When he opened it up there lay a boiled sweet in shiny gold paper, just waiting for her to pick it up. She loved when Señor Chavez visited because he always brought her a sweet.

'Sit down, Enrique. Isabel, bring us the bottle of wine.' José Mosca put his injured leg on the rickety wooden chair in front of him. The previous week he'd cut a hole in his foot with a pitchfork, and only made it home with the help of a passerby. He'd been in a bad mood ever since, and food was even scarcer than it had been before the accident. Señor Chavez had sent his son Antonio twice to José's field to keep the crops from going bad.

Isabel pocketed her sweet and went over to the cupboard to do as she had been told.

'I'm hoping to be back on my feet again next week. I'm going mad sitting here when there's so much to be done. If Señor Travez finds out someone else is working on the farm he could take it back; he probably will.'

'Not if you're back to normal soon. Besides, nobody knows but us.'

Isabel put a bowl of olives on the table and tried to open the wine bottle, but the cork was pushed in too tightly.

'Come here, Ratoncito. I will open it.'

'Ratoncito, that's a strange name for a daughter.' Señor Chavez looked between the two while José opened the bottle and poured them some wine.

'It's because she runs around with the energy of a mouse and eats everything she can find.'

Señor Chavez gave a loud belly laugh and Isabel felt her face go red. She glared at the mud floor until papá ruffled her dark hair, smiling for the first time in a week. 'Go and help your mamá now.'

She put her hand in her pocket to make sure the sweet was still there before reluctantly leaving the room. Instead of going to the back of the house where her mamá was washing clothes, Isabel sat on a large round stone just outside the window, where she could hear what was being discussed inside. The stone was warm from the days sun, and around it, the red soil of Andalucía cracked from lack of rain. She leaned back against the whitewashed stone house, listening to their voices. It wasn't that she was nosey, she just wanted to know what mood her papá would be in after Señor Chavez left. Also, she really didn't want to help with the washing.

'We need to dig up the weapons, José. All hell has broken lose in Madrid. The Guardia de Asalto have killed that bastard Sotelo in reprisal for the murder of José Castillo. We have to be able to defend ourselves.'

'There is always something, Enrique. We'll know if anything happens near here—then we'll dig up the weapons.'

'We know the rightwing Nationalist part of the army will try to get rid of our left-winged government, that much is clear, and the only way they can do that—seeing as they can't seem to get the majority of votes—is to overthrow it. I'm telling you, my friend, this is it; this is what will set it all off.'

'What if nothing happens and they find the weapons?'

'They don't need to be left in your house. I'll take them, if you'd like. The tension that has been building for decades, since long before the dictator Primo de Rivera came into power, is about to explode. It will happen any day, and when it does, we'd all better be ready.'

Isabel was losing interest and brought out the boiled sweet. The bright gold paper shimmered as she unwrapped it. Before she put it in her mouth, she held it up towards the July sun, trying to see through. When she grew up, she decided, she'd have lots of sweets in all different colours and in pretty wrapping. Then she'd go around handing them out to children who'd been good, and they would think she was the nicest person in the world.

'I would rather leave them where they are,' she heard papá say.

For a moment there was silence. 'We'll vote on it tonight then,' Señor Sanchez replied

There was a pause. 'I won't keep them in this house.'

'That's fine. I did say I'd take them. I suppose we'd better meet here rather than at Pedro's.'

'All right, but I feel very uneasy about it, Enrique. I'm as much an anarchist as anyone, but I don't want to see my family hurt. When you start bringing out guns and handing them to hotheads, which, let's face it, some of our members are, there is going to be trouble. Never mind what is going on in Madrid and Barcelona.'

'I know, but we didn't start this; we have to be able to protect ourselves if the right tries to take over the government. I have to go. Pilar will be cursing my name for missing dinner, and Antonio will be eager to get to the bar and see his friends.'

Isabel heard a chair scrape against the mud floor and just managed to hide behind the other side of the large stone before Señor Chavez came out.

His steps disappeared up the hillside and Isabel put half her sweet back in its wrapper for later.

That evening, the union members met at their house, and Isabel was told to go to bed so her mamá could join. Mamá had a lot of opinions on a lot of different matters, but normally never had the time to attend meetings with her husband. Only when they were held under her roof did she get a chance to make her views known.

Isabel lay on her straw mattress in the tiny room next to the kitchen but found there was no way she could possibly sleep. She could hear every word they uttered even before they started to raise their voices—which she knew they would as the meeting progressed.

'What are they talking about?' Luis asked his sister.

'You're not supposed to listen.'

'But I can hear them.'

'So don't listen then. Go to sleep.' She sighed, annoyed.

Her brother was due to start school in the autumn, and she was looking forward to a little time on her own. He was seven now and still under her charge, but whenever Isabel tried to do chores he would get in the way and she would be told off.

'I can't sleep. Will you tell me a story?'

'No. I'm trying to hear what they're saying. Stop talking.'

'But you said we weren't supposed to listen.'

'I said *you* weren't supposed listen. You're too young. I'll tell you a story tomorrow if you go to sleep.'

'All right, but don't forget,' he whispered, closing his eyes.

Satisfied, Isabel turned her attention back to the meeting.

'The government won't give us weapons to protect ourselves,' Enrique Chavez said. 'They are living in a different world. We can see what is happening all over this country. Any day now the right-wing Falangists and the church and all the rich men of Spain will try to take over the government. It is inevitable. If we don't distribute the weapons now we may never get another chance.' He paused long enough for effect, but not long enough to let anyone else speak. 'The landowner, De la Cruz, will crush us just like the Guardia Civil crushed the uprising at Casas Viejas in '33.

The church will denounce us, the Guardia Civil will kill us, and De la Cruz will take not just our land but everything else from us. I say we have no choice. Who's with me?'

Isabel thought he sounded pleased with himself and it seemed the majority agreed. Yet soon they fell silent and she could almost see him holding up a hand to quieten his comrades.

'My friends,' he continued, 'I'm not saying we should use them right now, but when the time comes it will give us a fair chance.' He paused and Isabel waited to hear what papá would say; mamá was shouting her support for Enrique.

After a long moment there came his voice, low and wary. 'Yes.'

'It's settled. Tomorrow, if convenient with you José, I will bring my son, Antonio, and we will dig up the weapons.'

Someone, one of the landless farm workers as Isabel could tell from his voice, started to shout passionately. 'I disagree. Let's take the weapons now and remove our enemies *tonight*. We know who they are, and we'll have the element of surprise. They have murdered enough of our comrades.'

Some murmured agreement, but Enrique managed to get regain everybody's attention. 'If we act now they will send the Guardia Civil in from Málaga. We need to time it right, keep a watchful eye for any sign of trouble rising from these people we know to be enemies of our cause and be prepared to move at a moment's notice. If we move in time with the rest of the unions across Spain, they won't be able to crush us so easily. Are we agreed? Good. Let's meet again in one week—unless anything happens in the meantime.'

The room slowly emptied, feet shuffling on the mud floor, as everybody gave their opinions, good or bad, to Enrique on their way out. Finally, silence fell and Isabel knew it was only the three of them left. Someone opened a cupboard and then came the sound of drinks being poured.

'You know they'll come after you if the other side gets to us first,' mamá said.

'They know we'll be stronger together, Maria, and thank you for agreeing about the weapons José. I think they respect you more than me,' Enrique said

'I don't agree with it at all,' said papá, and Isabel could tell he still stood from the closeness of his voice, 'but it's plain to see we're all headed for bloodshed of one kind or another, I'd rather it was theirs than ours.' There was a gentle scrape as he picked up his cup. '¡Salud! To the Republic, such as it is.'

***

The days after the meeting were tense, and Isabel wasn't sure what happened to the weapons they had been talking about or the enemies they mentioned. Papá's foot had almost healed, but he walked with a limp and it was decided that her mamá would work the field with him until Luis was old enough to take her place. In the meantime, now she was thirteen, all the household chores would fall onto Isabel's shoulders. She was not happy with the arrangement, but as everybody always kept on telling her: they were the lucky ones. At least they had somewhere to live and even though it wasn't much they always had something to eat; it was more than could be said for a lot of the other small farmers in the village. Worse off were the landless families, who had absolutely nothing and starved.

Out for a walk, Isabel bent over to pick a sprig of rosemary from one of the many bushes on the hillside and hurried past the Chavez's. At sixteen, Pilar was set to marry a distant cousin who lived within walking distance of her father's house. *Very clever*, Isabel thought, *as she can do the housework for both.* Maria had been to see her the previous week, and apparently Pilar couldn't talk about anything but her forthcoming wedding. As Señora Chavez had been dead for some time, Isabel's mamá felt she needed some female company before the wedding, and so Pilar spent quite a few afternoons at La Quida that summer of 1936.

Isabel tried to keep away whenever she was there; their talk of cooking and cleaning and children didn't interest her in the least. When she said as much, they both laughed as though she was still a small child and told her it one day would. The age difference between her and Pilar seemed a lot bigger just then, the years between thirteen and sixteen forming a line in the sand. Only a few years earlier, when Isabel had taught Pilar what she'd learned in school, their age difference hadn't seemed like such a big deal and she was surprised to find she missed those days. Now, they didn't have very much in common at all.

The wedding was booked for the end of July, so there was a whole week still to keep out of their way. Then, at least, Isabel wouldn't have to put up with Pilar's presence around the house and everything would go back to normal.

Yet she wasn't sure what that was as just that week the Nationalists (fascists, as her papá called them) had tried to overthrow the government—but her parents and the other union members were ready for them. Isabel didn't know what had happened down in the village, but the sound of gunshots echoed between the mountains every now and then. The mean landowners and their families had fled, and that was a good thing. On the odd occasion Isabel was allowed to walk down to the village she noticed a lot of men had guns and rifles, and there were red-and-black flags around the main square. The radio in her aunt and uncle's bar blared news, and her older cousins marched around the streets wearing their trade-union uniforms. They no longer had the time to play with her, which made her sad because she would very much have liked that part of her life to stay the same. Everything was changing, and as much as everybody seemed to agree this was a good thing, Isabel didn't. Her old teacher, Señor Sanchez, had been found guilty of being a fascist. She knew he'd been executed but couldn't understand why.

'Isabel, wait.' Pilar's voice echoed down the path behind her.

Isabel knew she should have run past the Chavez house instead of stopping nearby to pick rosemary. Now she was trapped.

'Hi, Pilar. I can't stop. There's so much....'

'Your parents are at our house. They asked me to get you. Come on.' Pilar started running back, and Isabel followed reluctantly.

As soon as she stepped into the crowded kitchen she felt the heavy atmosphere wrap itself around her. There were about twenty other men and women gathered, the men all wearing their CNT trade-union red-and-black neckerchiefs. Isabel assumed the rifles slung over their shoulders were those dug up a few weeks earlier. She spotted her parents in the corner, foreheads together and talking quietly. The radio could be heard in the background.

'What's happening?' She questioned Pilar but was unable to tear her gaze away from her parents.

'You're having another baby brother or sister.'

Isabel looked around, shocked. 'Is that what all this is about?'

'No, you silly girl. The army generals have tried to overthrow the government, so now we all have to fight.'

'Who are fighting?'

'Our men, and some of the women too. Both our fathers are going. If they let me I'll go, too.'

Isabel left Pilar where she was standing and walked up to her papá. 'Is it true? Are you leaving?'

José let go of his wife and looked at his daughter. 'I am, but only for a short time. We can't let the fascists take over the country, now can we? You understand, don't you, Ratoncito?'

Isabel nodded even though she didn't understand—at all. 'Do you promise to come back soon?'

'Of course; I will.'

Even though she now came up to his shoulders, papá lifted her off her feet with a hug before putting her down again.

'You'll have to work very hard while I'm not here. This is our land and we must look after it. Especially now that you have a little baby brother or sister coming.' He put his work-worn hand on his wife's stomach before looking over towards the door. Enrique was calling him over. 'I'm sorry, I have to go now.' He slung his rifle across his shoulders and followed the rest out the door, turning around to smile and wave at her. Then he was gone.

It had all happened so fast. Isabel didn't run outside to wave goodbye like her mamá and Luis did; she just stood where her papá had put her down, staring at the doorway through which he'd disappeared. Afterwards, she wished she had.

***

Her papá was gone for over two months. So many rumours of death and defeat were passed around that his family were constantly worried. Then, in September, he finally returned. José looked tired and drawn, and still wore the same clothes in which he'd left.

'Where did you go, papá?' Isabel asked the question as they all sat together on a couple of old wine barrels, looking out over the valley and mountains ahead.

'He's been fighting the fascists,' Luis answered on his behalf, smug.

'I was talking to my papá, not to you.' She glared at her brother before turning her attention back to her papá. It felt as though he'd been away for years, not just a couple of months. There had been a lack of togetherness since he left, as if the three remaining family members had simply bided their time while waiting for him to return. All the village farmland and cattle were now communal, and everybody had to work the land. For families like theirs—those whose primary worker had left to fight—this arrangement worked well enough, as they would have had trouble doing all the work on their own. All food was collected by the committee and shared equally amongst all the families. The war had only started in July yet there hadn't been much food, so they lived on what they could forage in the hills and ate meat from the cattle confiscated from the old landowner. Once all the crops were harvested they would be all right, Isabel believed.

'Don't you two start fighting, now,' mamá said, angry. 'Your papá doesn't want to listen to that.'

'I hope you've been good while I've been away. I can't worry about what your mamá has to put up with as well as killing fascists.' He smiled at the last word and put his arm around his son.

'I knew it,' Luis beamed.

Isabel felt ignored by his preferential treatment of Luis and felt this moment, which she'd been waiting for ever since he left, was ruined. She couldn't let them see how upset she was, and as hot tears flowed down her cheeks Isabel ran to one of her secret hiding places, sitting down on the dry mud under the low branches of a pine tree. Suddenly, she felt ashamed of her behaviour. She was thirteen years old and was acting like a child. Yet the thought of having to apologise to them all made her cry again. She jumped a little at the appearance of her papá's face between the pine boughs.

He looked around the small space before entering and sat down next to her. 'What's wrong, Ratoncito? Aren't you happy I'm back home?'

Isabel managed to stop crying and threw her arms around his neck. 'I *am* glad you're home, papá. I'm so sorry. I've just missed you so much.'

José peeled his daughter's arms from his neck and held her shoulders. 'You have to stop thinking about just yourself now. Your mamá has to be able to rely on your help. Do you understand?'

She nodded. 'I just missed you, that's all.'

'I missed you, too. So, are you going to tell me what you've been up to since I left, or will I have to ask your brother about it?'

They both burst into laughter and by the time she'd told him everything it had grown dark outside the hideaway surrounded by pines.

Over the following days Isabel and Luis hardly saw their parents. They both left for the village in the early morning and didn't return until late. Isabel could hear them talking long into the night.

'I've been quite safe in Málaga, but the things I've done, Maria. The things we've all done.' His voice trailed off and there was silence until he continued. 'It had to be done, and that's that.'

'What did you do?' mamá asked. 'What can be so bad?'

'I can't tell you. It was madness. People were tried and shot by the hundreds. In a lot of cases there wasn't even a trial.'

'But they're fascists,' mamá replied. 'They would have done it to you.'

'Some were, but some were just denounced by people who didn't like them. It's calmed down now, but the trials are still ongoing.'

'We're at war now. It was never going to be easy.'

'No, but I didn't think there would be indiscriminate killings. Everybody, including me, are afraid of saying or doing the wrong thing.'

'We will beat them though, won't we?'

'I don't know. Nobody knows. I hope so, Maria, but the news from the front line, and from the towns that have been captured by Franco and his army, are worse than your worst nightmare.'

'Worse than Málaga?'

'Yes. Much worse than Málaga. They have modern weapons and airplanes they've received from Germany and Italy, along with the soldiers to operate them. Our soldiers consider themselves lucky if they have bullets for their ancient guns and rifles. The Nationalists have taken town after town on their way to Madrid and only a couple of days ago they took Ronda. That's only forty kilometres from here, Maria. I don't want to scare you, but in the towns and cities they take they kill everybody: men, women, children; they don't need much of an excuse. If they get close to the village, you must take the children and go to Málaga. At least it's bigger, and if the worst happens you can hide.'

'How will I know, José? How will I know where they are? And where would we go in Málaga?'

'Go into the village every day, or send Isabel for news. There is a family in Málaga I've got to know. They're very helpful, and union members too. The wife, Señora Araya, wrote down their address for me so that, if needed, you and the children would have somewhere to stay—and I would be able to find you.'

'But how will *I* find it? I don't know how to read.'

'I know, but if you need to leave the farm you can always ask directions to Málaga. Then, when you get there, you can show somebody who can read the note and they'll you where to go.'

'Let's hope it doesn't come to that. I would like our new baby born here on the farm, where he belongs.'

'That might not happen. I just want you and the children to be safe.'

'Surely they don't just kill everybody in the towns. There must be a court to decide?'

'Maria, they've never needed a court for permission to kill us. Now they have free rein to do what they like and call it war; they've gone mad. Hundreds upon hundreds, maybe even thousands, killed for having voted for the Republic or for carrying a union card—women, children, anyone.'

'Like what we're doing to their side now?' mamá's voice was hard. 'I'm sorry, I didn't mean that.'

Isabel heard a chair scrape the floor and quickly disappeared under her blanket before the bedroom door opened and her father came in.

She heard him move about before laying down on their mattress in the far corner. Shortly afterwards her mamá came in and she could feel her eyes on her. 'Go to sleep, Isabel,' she whispered, and lay down next to her husband.

He left early on the third morning. After an emotional goodbye José walked down the path towards the village, where he was catching a lift back to his unit. Isabel took some comfort in what he had said about Málaga being safe, and that they could join him there if things got bad. She'd also heard what he said about the killings of civilians, and her stomach formed a knot. She found herself looking for fascists every time her eyes wandered to the tops of the mountains surrounding their home. Where were they? If they came here, would they kill her and her family? At night when she went to bed Isabel told Luis stories of little birds and animals, full of happy things, to distract her own mind and allow herself to sleep with calm thoughts. She didn't tell mamá about her worries because she didn't want to add to her troubles, and she'd promised papá she would be good and helpful. So that was exactly what she would be. She no longer waited to be asked to do the washing or to weed the vegetable field. Rather, she volunteered to go to the village and help with anything she could, although she did have an ulterior motive: She wanted to be the first to hear any news so she could run home to warn mamá.

So it was that one October day, while in the village, Isabel met Pilar. She'd left to get married shortly after the troops had left for Málaga in July, and she hadn't been back since. It hadn't been a big wedding with lots of celebrations as it should have been because of what was happening in Spain. Instead, Pilar had come to La Quida to say goodbye before leaving with Antonio for her fiancée's village. Her brother had returned a few days later, now living alone in the Chavez house.

Pilar had changed so much in the few short months since she had left that Isabel hardly recognised her.

'Isabel! It's been a long time since we last met.'

Isabel wanted to tell her the blue overalls she wore didn't suit her, but she had promised to be good and she was sticking to it.

Pilar smiled and pointed towards a man in militia clothing on the other side of the street. 'That's my husband over there. Come, I'll introduce you.'

Isabel couldn't come up with an excuse not to. 'You look very different.' She glanced at Pilar's dark hair, which was now considerably shorter than it used to be. Her clothes looked more suited for a man than a woman.

Pilar laughed and took Isabel's arm, walking her across the main street towards her husband. 'Yes, I suppose I do. I've joined the CNT militia—just like our papás and my husband. I've already been fighting for our freedom.'

'You've fought real soldiers? But you're a girl.'

'Women can do anything now. You are such a country girl, Isabel. We can vote and fight and do anything we want. I don't really like the short hair, but you don't want it falling into your face while you're shooting. And you're more likely to catch lice, too, if your hair is long.'

At the mention of lice Isabel stopped and withdrew the hand Pilar had taken hold of.

'I haven't got lice now, but we were at the western front before we came back here, and in the trenches, they were crawling everywhere. Well, that's the least of our problems. I won't tell you more because you'll have nightmares.' She stopped next to a man much older than her, who had a thick dark moustache that looked as though it had been glued onto his face rather than grown there naturally. 'Isabel, this is my husband, Señor Murillo.'

Isabel mumbled a greeting which seemed to fall on deaf ears, as Pilar's husband turned his attention straight back to whom he was talking.

Pilar looked a little embarrassed and after a few moments they walked back up the road. 'He's very busy, I'm afraid.'

'That's all right. Do you want to come and say hello to mamá? She would like to see you.' Isabel could have bitten off her own tongue for uttering those words, but once again she'd felt a little sorry for Pilar. When Isabel got married, her husband would always listen to her and take her advice. He would not have a moustache and he would not be rude.

'I can't right now, but we're staying at my father's house until things settle down. I'll come and see her as soon as I can.'

'What do you mean "until things settle down"? Until we've won?'

'Maybe, but before then we have to organise protection of this area. Our enemy is not far from here and they move so quickly they could be here in a couple of days if they wanted. Isabel, where are you going?'

Isabel ran all the way up the mountain, past the crossroads and along the path up to their house. Her lungs felt as if they would explode by the time she got home. Her mamá, startled by her daughter's sudden appearance, dropped the hoe she was using and ran up to her.

'What's happened? Is your father all right?'

Isabel could only nod as she caught her breath. 'The fascists could be here in two days, mamá. We must leave. Now.'

'Who told you this?'

'Pilar. She's joined the militia and she and her new husband are here to protect the village.'

Mamá's shoulders relaxed a little. 'Pilar is here to protect the village? I don't know if I should laugh or cry. Either she is exaggerating, or the government doesn't think much of us out here.' She took off her apron and strode towards the village. 'Either way, we need to know what's happening. Look after your brother and finish the weeding.' She shouted these last instructions over her shoulder before disappearing up the path.

When she returned a short while later, she declared they were leaving for Málaga the following day. She couldn't get a clear answer from anyone, but Franco had set himself up as Caudillo of all of Spain earlier that week and Maria wanted to be with her husband.

What she said didn't make sense, but Isabel didn't argue. Instead, she set about helping mamá to pack whatever they could carry. They would bury anything valuable in the garden.

In the box they used to store vegetables they carefully placed the oil lamp that had always been in the kitchen but never lit, papa's glass he always drank wine from when he was home, and other little things that fit. They didn't have much, but these were their family's treasures and had to be kept safe as they couldn't bring them along.

Mamá sprinkled seeds, then covered them with mud and a few stones to hide any signs of their digging.

'I'd like to see someone steal that from us,' she said as Isabel and Luis put the last stones in place.

~ 3 ~

**Andalucía, Spain
February 2003**

'Has your mamá told you much about her life?' Peter asked.

Mapi was at first quiet as they drove towards the site. It had clouded over, and the car's heater blasted hot air that dried out her contact lenses. They were finally going to the grave site. She was anxious to get there; Peter had forgotten his laptop at the hotel and the five-minute drive turned into forty-five.

'No. Not much anyway. I do know my grandfather, José, is believed to be buried in this mass grave. I found out a few things about her early life from her brother and some of her later life from my father. Only general things, though. My father said I was too young to know everything, but then I moved to Málaga to go to university and forgot all about it. He died almost ten years ago now. My uncle lives in Alicante and he doesn't like to talk about anything involving mamá. I suspect they had a big fallout at some point, but she still worships him—or, rather, the memory of him. They haven't met in many years.'

'With this line of work, I've found that people tend to form barriers with their memories. Sometimes it helps to talk things through with a professional,' Peter said.

Mapi laughed out loud. 'The only professional that would make mamá open up would be a professional hitman. I'm sorry, that was a bad joke. I was born in the forties and grew up under Franco, but because I didn't know any different, I didn't have anything to complain about. I knew my parents didn't like him, even though they never said it out loud. In school we were taught the '36-'39 war was fought against foreign communists, not brother against brother. We believed it because, well, why wouldn't we?'

'So, if I put on the tape recorder can you explain, before we get to the site, the background to this and other exhumations being done around Spain?'

'Sure.' She waited for the recorder to start before continuing. 'During the Spanish Civil War, and its aftermath, an estimated 300,000 people died on the battlefields and a further 200,000 Republicans were executed. The figures vary because there aren't many records. Most people were killed and thrown into unmarked mass graves, or they died in prison work camps. The only reason we know now where some of the grave sites are located is due to villagers who know their location—though most are still too scared to show much of an interest. After Franco's death in 1975 both the left and the right formed the Pact of Forgetting, *Pacto del olvido*, and agreed to protect the criminals who had committed these crimes.' Mapi continued, explaining Spain's transition from an autocracy to a democracy; it was a history she'd only found out about a few years ago herself. 'This is a vibrant country and its politics are still a very passionate subject, but the Pact of Forgetting allowed Spain a calm route back to democracy. However, this meant those who had been silenced and brainwashed for so many years still do not have a chance to tell their stories, or to find out what happened to their fathers, their mothers, or their other relatives.'

'But now that is all changing, right?' Peter asked, ever the producer. 'That's why they're digging up these graves.'

'In a way. It only started in 2000 and this organisation, the one overseeing this dig, is staffed by volunteers and funded mostly by donations. The government is not overly involved. They'll pay to bring home bodies of those who fell in other parts of Europe while fighting for Germany during the Second World War, but they won't take an active part in recovering those who died on their own soil by their own hands.'

'That's probably fine for now,' Peter said, putting the recorder back in his pocket. 'It would be good to get a personal view on it all from you; not right now, but maybe later.' He relaxed back in his seat. 'Why did you get involved? I know your family is connected to the war, but so are most families here in one way or another. What made you want to become a crusader for truth?'

Mapi laughed. 'That's not quite how I see myself. I had the pleasure of showing Simon Ulridge, the historian, around Madrid some years ago now. He was a lovely man, and I showed him what I thought to be our history. Bearing in mind I'm a journalist based in Madrid—albeit up to that point I had mainly reported on foreign news—I thought I knew it well. Turned out that Simon knew the fundamentals much better, and I felt thoroughly ashamed of my ignorance. Once I started looking into the war, I became obsessed with the whole thing. So much so the paper I worked for found me less and less work. I left and started working for a variety of other papers, writing not just about the lost history of Spain but also about people's lives. About people like me who grew up in a vacuum of ignorance, were fed lies in school, and heard only silence at home. Of course, this didn't happen to everybody: some families talked—in hushed voices behind closed doors—about what happened, but the shame inflicted upon those who supported the Republicans made many unwilling to talk to even their own children or grandchildren. My generation, and my daughter's generation, deserves to know their true history and not to be afraid to speak of the past.' She shrugged her shoulders and looked out of the window. 'We're here now.'

The car stopped by the sign marking the exhumation site, and they stepped out onto the mud track. It was quite early in the morning and therefore no curious onlookers had yet arrived. At other sites she had visited, or worked on as a volunteer, local interest always grew the longer they were there. It started with a few glances, then some would come for a closer look, and towards the end of the dig there would be stories written down in the visitor's book or longer versions told behind closed doors, out of sight of the rest of the village, to the volunteers who recorded every word.

Mapi had often visited this particular site with her mamá, but she was never told why they'd driven here rather than to the park. She would watch her mamá sit in silence, her back towards a pine tree, and wonder what she was thinking. When she did ask, her mamá would smile at her, sadness in her eyes, and say this is where she came to remember what had been, and one day, when Mapi was grown-up, she would tell her about it. Yet so far she hadn't. One time her mamá had taken her further up the road that led between two towering mountains. It must have been springtime because she'd shown Mapi a valley full of wild asparagus. She'd laughed and told her about other secret places she'd had while she was a child. Mapi remembered being so happy then, not because of the asparagus, but because mamá had laughed so easily.

'Mapi, it's good to see you again.' The dig coordinator she had been working with for the last year came out from the large tent that had been erected near the site.

'Gil, it's good to see you too. These are the members of the British documentary crew I told you about.' She introduced them, and he and Peter shook hands. 'I've explained to them a little of what you do in general, but maybe you could explain in more detail so they can get all their facts correct.'

'Of course. I'll show you where we are with the exhumation first, so you get a sense of what we do before we move on to the background information.' Gil started walking, pointing towards the areas that had been cordoned off.

Heart beating fast, Mapi followed. This could be the place where her family history lay buried.

While Mapi dug into her past Isabel looked up from the photo of her papá and shivered. She'd grown cold from sitting still too long. Putting the photo down on the bed she went over to the window. Through the cracks in the shutters she could see sunlight and thought she should maybe sit in the back garden for a little while to warm up. The shutters would normally be open, but since she had fell and hurt her back the previous month, she could only open them from the outside. Besides, she hadn't wanted to leave the house until this business with the film crew had been settled. It was silly, really, and she knew it. Times had changed and nothing bad would happen to her now just because her daughter wanted people to know their history.

Isabel admired Mapi, just like she'd admired Pilar in the end. It was noble to stand up for what you believed to be right, no matter what anyone tried to do to stop you. She went back to her bed and put the photo back in the drawer. Before her daughter returned to Madrid, she'd make sure she knew everything about her history. It was only fair she knew about their past. *Well, most of it.* There were some things Isabel had tried to forget for sixty-four years, but still those memories surfaced when she least expected.

~ 4 ~

**Andalucía, Spain
October 1936**

When they left the house the following morning, wearing every bit of clothing they owned, the night's chill hadn't yet lifted. Isabel wore her Sunday dress pulled over her everyday dress, and it was all rather tight. Mamá had packed the few bits of food they had left, some bedding, and a photograph of her husband which she had taken to keeping in her pocket. She hid her pregnancy under the loose grey dress she wore, and if you didn't know you would never notice.

Isabel stopped and turned just before their home, La Quida, went out of view. She thought it looked sad to see them leave, already dark and damp, although in her mind it had always been full of life and sunshine. As happy as she was that they were going to find papá, she was also sad to leave.

'Don't worry Isabel, we'll be back soon,' mamá said when she noticed her daughter had stopped. 'See this as an adventure. I promise you that no matter who wins this war we will always have La Quida. Its soil is in our blood, and we belong here.' She took her daughter's hand and pulled her along. 'Come on, now. We have a long way to go before nightfall.'

Requisitioned cars and trucks full of soldiers were arriving in the village as they walked past. Guns on their laps and cigarettes in their mouths, the soldiers chatted and laughed as the trucks came to a standstill. Isabel scoured their faces to see if papá was amongst them, only to be disappointed.

'Is the road to Málaga safe?' mamá asked of one.

'We've just come from there, and it's all clear for now,' he replied.

'My husband is stationed there. José Mosca. Do you know him? He's also CNT.'

'No. I'm sorry. We only passed through. Good luck.'

He turned and walked with the rest of his comrades towards the town hall, where the new CNT headquarters had been set up.

'Well, at least the road is safe,' mamá said, and they started walking southeast.

'Do you know where we're going, mamá?' Luis asked

'I know the general direction. I went to Málaga once when I was a girl. My grandfather took me on his horse. It was a big and dirty town, and I was pleased when we went home, but I had a lovely time with my grandfather.'

'I've never been past the road down there.' Isabel pointed towards the far end of the road they were on. 'Do you think I will find it big and dirty, too?'

'I don't know. Maybe.'

'If it's not very nice, why do people live there?'

'They live there because that's where they can find work. Some work on the big ships that come and go from the harbour. They sail all over the world.'

'I'd like to go on one of those,' Luis said.

'On a ship?' mamá asked.

'Yes.'

'Luis, what is a ship?' Isabel asked, knowing full well he didn't know.

He shrugged his shoulders. 'Things that take you places, so you don't have to walk.'

'You're stupid,' Isabel said, laughing. 'Everybody knows what a ship is.'

'Isabel, stop it. There will be no more talking until I say so. Do you understand?' mamá chided her without slowing down.

They both nodded, but Luis stuck out his tongue. Isabel pretended she didn't see because she had just remembered she was supposed to be good.

After a couple of hours of walking their feet had started to blister. Apart from using some soft leaves to protect the blisters from rubbing against their shoes, there was nothing they could do. Every step hurt. Isabel wanted to take off her shoes and walk barefoot, but mamá wouldn't let her.

'If you think those blisters are bad, just imagine your feet worn away to the bone by these stones. If that's what you want, then take them off.'

When she put it like that it was easier to put up with the pain, yet by the end of the day Isabel's feet were so numb that they no longer hurt. The hunger pained, however, and she knew the other's felt it too.

Trucks and cars sometimes passed, but the mountain roads were mostly quiet. They walked in silence, stopping at villages or houses by the roadside for water to drink. Always there was someone who wanted to know who they were and from where they'd come.

'How much further do we have to go?' Isabel asked. She sat beside mamá on a fallen tree in the clearing where they'd stopped for the night. The sun was setting and the air was cold, but they were too tired and too hungry to care. As soon as they sat down their numb feet turned into lumps of pain.

'I don't know,' came the brusque reply. mamá handed them each a small piece of bread with some pickled cauliflower. 'That's all you get I'm afraid.' Isabel thought she looked as if she might cry. 'You can have an apple afterwards. I wish I could give you more, but I don't know how long it will take us to get to Málaga and find your father.'

Isabel noticed she hadn't taken anything for herself. 'What are you going to eat?'

'I will eat when you two are asleep.'

'Don't cry. Please, mamá, have my apple. I don't need it.' She edged closer and took her hand. 'It will all be all right. We just need to find papá.'

'I know,' she replied, squeezing her daughter's hand. 'Go on and eat up while I unpack the blankets. It will get even colder tonight.'

Luis had finished his bread and sat looking between his mamá and his sister, not quite sure what to do. In the end he decided to stay where he was and concentrate on the apple he had been given.

The night was long and cold, and even though Isabel was tired, she couldn't sleep. They'd huddled together for warmth, but apart from the odd doze, the only one who slept through until morning was Luis. Isabel was asleep as the sun rose, and when she woke, her mamá was gone.

She sat up and looked around, yet there was no sign of her. Panic started to rise and Isabel thought that maybe mamá had left them there, or a wild animal had taken her.

'Mamá. Mamá, where are you?' Her voice was shrill with worry.

'Why are you shouting?' Luis had been woken by his sister's cries.

Isabel ignored him and got up from under the blanket. Mamá wouldn't have left them; she would have gone to find more food or water. She walked up to the road, but there was no sign of her. Her bag was still there, and Isabel knew she wouldn't have left it unless she'd been kidnapped.

'Where's mamá?' Luis asked, his eyes wide at his sister's manic running around.

'She's gone to find some food. Go back to sleep.'

'You don't know where she is, or you wouldn't be shouting.'

'Be quiet, Luis. We'll sit here and wait for her to return.'

'I'm hungry.'

'We're all hungry. We can't eat anything until mamá comes back.'

Just then they saw her walking back up the road wearing a smile. 'Look what I found!' She held out a large loaf of bread in one hand and some cheese in the other.

'Where did you find it? On the road?'

She smiled at Luis. 'No, silly boy. A kind woman gave it to me.'

Isabel felt as though she would burst into tears. 'I thought you'd gone.'

Mamá came and stood beside her. 'If I could, I would lift you up and give you a hug. I would die before I left you. It just took a little longer than I thought to find some food.' She sat down between them and gave them careful portions. When they were done, they packed up the blanket and food and again started walking towards the coast.

That afternoon they got their first glimpse of the sea. When they were a bit closer, they stopped to watch the afternoon sun shimmer upon the water's surface. Isabel thought she'd never seen anything quite so beautiful. From where she was standing, Málaga didn't seem dirty at all.

They reached Málaga just as the sun sank behind the sea. Militia roamed the streets and strange smells hung in the air. The gravel roads they'd walked on so far changed to cobblestones, which Isabel found difficult to walk on. She couldn't stop looking at the unfamiliar surroundings, and just managed to jump out of the way when a bicycle nearly ran her over. With tired legs and sore feet, they found someone to give directions to the house papá had told them to find.

'It's not too far from here, but it's a dangerous city after dark. Fascists roam the streets carrying guns, and people tend to shoot before asking questions. I'll take you to the house you seek.'

The old man had hair as fluffy and white as a cloud, and he smelled like a faint memory Isabel had of her grandfather smoking a pipe in front of the fire. His clothes were full of holes, as were his rope shoes. Isabel could see one of his large toes sticking out.

They stumbled past rows of houses, their windows blacked out, and from nearby came the sound of gunfire.

'They've caught someone, I reckon,' the old man said.

'A fascist?' Luis asked.

'Indeed,' the old man replied. 'Back in the summer, the streets were full of militias bringing people in for questioning—'

'Thank you, Señor, but I think my children will have nightmares as it is.'

'I beg your pardon, Señora. It's easy to forget that some children are still ... children.' He marched through the dark, almost deserted streets as they tried to keep up. They followed him down narrow, pebbled roads until, finally, he stopped. 'Here it is.' He paused before offering kindly, 'I'll stay and make sure somebody is here.'

The once-whitewashed terraced house looked as dark and empty as the street in which it stood. Gone was the bustle of the main part of the city, but they could still hear distant traffic and, closer, the cries of seagulls from the seafront at the end of the road.

'Thank you. That's very kind of you,' mamá said as she walked up the stone steps to the front door. She hesitated before knocking, not liking to disturb anybody at this time of night. Yet, as there was no other choice, she knocked quietly on the door. Isabel hoped it was the right address. When there was no answer mamá knocked louder, and the door finally opened. A pale, solemn face peeked out. The girl was small, and her light brown hair hung loose around her shoulders.

'Is this the house of Señora Araya?' mamá asked. The child just looked at her.

A woman's voice shouted from inside. 'Who is it?'

'We're friends of Señora Araya. We're very tired. Is she here?'

The little girl closed the door and mamá knocked again. A long moment later a pale young woman in dirty clothes opened the door. Her auburn hair also hung long and lose over her shoulders. 'You're looking for Señora Araya?'

'Yes. My husband told me to find her when we came to Málaga. Is she here?'

The woman shook her head. 'No. She is at a meeting and won't be back for a few hours.'

'We were told we could stay with her. May we wait for her inside?'

'I'm not sure...'

'Please. We have nowhere else to go. If Señora Araya wants us to leave when she gets home, we'll go.'

After a few moments the woman moved out of the way. 'All right, come in.'

Mamá ushered Isabel and Luis inside before turning towards the man who had shown them the way.

'Gracias, Comrade. I wish I had something to give you for your help.'

'You're welcome. I hope the Señora is as accommodating as you think. These are hard times, and there are a lot of refugees in the town. You may have trouble finding another place to stay.'

With that he turned and walked back in the direction they'd come. Mamá stepped into the dark hallway and closed the door. Isabel thought the house smelled of nothing, as if nobody lived there. Their home had always smelled clean, and of something cooking or put out to soak.

The tall woman, whose name was Irena, turned out to be the mother of the small child. They, too, were staying there as friends of Señora Araya. Irena showed them into a small lounge on the ground floor and asked them to sit on an old green sofa while they waited. She lit a couple of candles so they could see. The fireplace remained unlit, and in the flickering light from the candles Isabel could just make out the faces of the others.

Irena called to them from the doorway. 'Have you got any food with you?'

'Only a small piece of bread,' answered mamá.

Irena nodded slowly. 'That's a shame. My girl hasn't eaten for two days. It's not easy, here in the city. You'd have been better off staying in the countryside.'

Mamá looked up at Irena from where she sat. 'There's no need for you to wait with us if you need to sleep.' There was a sternness in her voice that didn't escape Irena's attention.

'I guess so. I will trust you, seeing as Señora Araya has sold everything of any value anyway.' She threw a quick look at the big bag mamá had placed on the floor in front of her before stepping out of the room and walking upstairs.

Isabel sat on the sofa, her feet dangling. After the hard ground the night before, the sofa felt soft and she could hardly keep her eyes open. Luis was already sleeping, his head leaning against her arm. After their long and tiring journey, it felt good to be out of the cold.

'Will the Señora let us stay here like papá said?' Isabel fought against sleep.

'Of course she will. Now go to sleep, Isabel.'

Her eyes had already closed. 'Will you wake me if papá arrives?'

'He doesn't know we're here yet.'

'But if he does?'

'Yes. I'll wake you up if he comes.'

As soon as she heard those words Isabel allowed herself to go to sleep.

***

The following morning, when Isabel woke and looked around, it took her a little while to remember where she was. The wooden shutters were closed, but light came in thorough the cracks and she could hear people outside the window, talking loudly as they passed. She was alone, but she could hear Luis's voice from the other side of the closed lounge door. From behind it also came the scent of something cooking.

Satisfied she wasn't on her own, Isabel neatly folded the blanket mamá must have covered her with after she fell asleep. She put it back in the bag that still stood where mamá had sat the previous evening before walking towards the door. It opened into a kitchen with a small wooden table and a single cupboard. Like the lounge in which they'd slept there were brown tiles on the floor, and the room was dully lit by the sunshine struggling to get through the dirty glass windows. Steam from a pot on the stove swirled towards the ceiling.

Her brother was sitting at the table together with the little girl who had opened the door when they'd first arrived. She wore a dress that had at some point been blue but was now a light shade of grey and thin with wear. They both had a bowl of watery soup in front of them. By the dirty window stood the woman who'd let them in. Irena. She had a cigarette in her hand and ill-smelling plumes of smoke hung in the air.

When she noticed Isabel she sighed and went over to the saucepan on the stove. 'Do you want some breakfast?'

Isabel nodded. 'Yes, please. Do you know where our mamá is?'

'Yes.' Irena put her cigarette out on a plate. 'She went out with the Señora this morning to find her husband. I was left here, as usual. Sit down.' She pointed to a chair next to her daughter. 'What's your name?'

'It's Isabel.'

Irena put down a bowl of grainy stock. 'How old are you, Isabel?'

'I'm thirteen.'

'You're almost a grown-up, wouldn't you say?'

Isabel nodded as she put a spoonful of the soup in her mouth. It was hot, but she didn't know what it was, and it left a funny taste in her mouth. She looked at Luis, who had finished his soup and was getting restless. Irena took his and her daughter's bowls away and placed them by the sink.

'I have to go out for a little while, so you'll have to wait here for your mamá. You can look after them, can't you, Isabel.' It wasn't a question. 'I'll be back soon.' Irena threw Isabel a slightly crooked smile before rushing out the door before she had a chance to object.

Well, what else was new? Isabel always ended up with the bad jobs. She'd much rather have gone looking for papá than stay here and babysit Luis and someone whose name she didn't even know.

'What's your name?' she asked her. The girl looked up but didn't answer. 'If you don't tell me I'm going to have to call you "Quiet Girl", and that's not very pretty.'

Still, she didn't answer. Isabel sighed before picking up her bowl and putting the contents back in the saucepan. It was awful. She'd ask mamá if she had any more bread or pickles when she returned. She was excited mamá had gone to get papá, as then they could stay with him and not in this dirty house.

Isabel didn't want the Señora, whom she was still to meet, to be embarrassed about the state of the house when her papá arrived, so she looked around and found some water and some rags, but no soap; she'd have to work with what she had. She would heat the water and scrub harder than she normally would, and thought the rosemary twigs she had in her bag would make the house smell nice. It might even smell a bit like home.

After checking on Luis, who had found a box of playing cards and was building something out of them on the floor in the lounge, the quiet girl watching his every move, Isabel opened the window to let some air into the kitchen. She then filled a bucket and rubbed her rosemary twigs into the water.

As she scrubbed the floor she sang 'Torre mi Amigo' at the top of her voice and hummed 'A las Barricadas' as she cleaned the windows. She drew looks from passersby, curious as to who this happy, singing girl was. Some smiled and Isabel smiled back, whilst others just wandered past, lost in their own thoughts. Luis came to the doorway to see what she was doing, holding his fingers in his ears. She ignored him.

Isabel could only conclude that the happiness she felt was because papá was nearby, and he would make everything all right. They would be back home in no time at all, so she might as well enjoy being here as she would probably never get the chance to be in Málaga again.

'I want to go out, Isabel,' Luis said a little while later when he'd got fed up with trying to entice the quiet girl to play games. 'I want to see the ships.'

'I don't know where they are, and we don't want to get lost.'

'Please.'

Isabel thought it over for a minute. If they only walked a few streets away they'd easily be able to find their way back. She knew mamá wouldn't approve, but she was the grown-up here and could make the decisions.

'Okay. But not far. If the ships are further than a short walk from here, you'll have to wait for mamá.'

'What about her?' Luis pointed towards the girl standing beside him.

'She can come with us, but she'll need something warmer to wear.' Isabel took the girl's hand and walked up the stairs. 'You stay down here, Luis.'

When they got to the first floor, she looked at the girl.

'Which room are you staying in?'

The girl walked into a room on the left.

'So, you understand what I say but you won't talk to me. Oh, well. Have you got anything else to wear?'

The girl shook her head.

'That's all you have? It's all torn and full of holes. You can't go out like that.'

Isabel walked back downstairs, the girl following behind, just as mamá walked in through the front door. She was accompanied by with another woman. 'Did you find him?' she asked eagerly.

Mamá took a deep breath and shook her head. 'No. He's left Málaga. Some say he's gone to help keep the Badajoz line, and some say he's gone to help keep the Madrid line. Nobody seems to know exactly where he is but said if they find out they'll let us know. I'm not holding my breath.'

The woman behind mamá spoke up. 'They'll find him. Everybody's on the move now, so it takes a little time for the paperwork to catch up.'

'Señora Araya, this is my daughter Isabel, and this boy here is my son, Luis. Children, this is Señora Araya. This is her house.'

Isabel and Luis said hello. The girl with no name stood quietly next to Isabel on the bottom step.

'Papá isn't here?' Luis said, disappointed. 'But we can't go back home because I haven't seen the ships yet.'

'Don't worry, little Señor,' Señora Araya said. 'You can stay here for a few days, or longer, until we find out his whereabouts. You will see the ships.'

'Thank you,' mamá said. 'That's very kind of you.'

As long as you don't mind sleeping in there.' She pointed towards the lounge where they'd spent the night before. 'I would offer you the room upstairs, but Irena wouldn't take too kindly to being moved.' Señora Araya sniffed the air. 'Is that rosemary I can smell? Someone has been busy cleaning, and I don't think it was my other lodger. Thank you, Isabel.'

Isabel could only nod. A lump had formed in her throat as mamá had spoken about papá, and if she opened her mouth she'd burst into tears. She'd been so happy earlier. Why couldn't he just be here? He had said he would.

'Why don't we go back home? He might be there,' Luis said.

'We can't. There's been reports of battles taking place just on the other side of the mountains. We'd just be walking straight into trouble. No ... we'll take advantage of

Señora Araya's hospitality for a few days, and then we'll see. We'll be perfectly fine here.'

The two women had managed to get some onions and potatoes, which they cooked with the rest of Isabel's rosemary. After the meal mamá and Señora Araya went out again, and Isabel was once again alone with the two younger ones. Irena hadn't yet come home. Earlier, the Señora had asked where she was, but did not seem surprised she'd left her daughter.

'That woman needs to take responsibility for herself and her child,' she'd said while putting on her coat.

'Why is she staying here, Señora?' Luis had asked.

'She's a friend of a friend.'

'Why is Quiet Girl so quiet? She won't even tell us her name.'

'Her name is Rosa, and she's not deaf so don't talk about her as if she's not here.'

Luis went quiet and looked down at the floor.

'We don't know why she won't talk.' Señora Araya then turned to the quiet girl. 'Why don't you talk to us, cariño?'

Rosa had just looked at them, her eyes as deep and dark as the well at La Quida.

'Some day, maybe you can tell us why.' The Señora had bent down and kissed Rosa's cheek before leaving the house, mamá in tow.

The following weeks followed the same pattern, and they saw less of mamá than they ever had. She went out with Señora Araya, and Isabel didn't have a clue as to what they did all day. She hoped they were trying to find a way for them to go back home to the farm, with papá. Irena continued to take advantage of Isabel's presence and left the house after breakfast every day, only returning late at night.

Isabel, Luis, and Rosa went exploring around the town, and could often be found watching the big ships in the harbour, making up stories of where they'd been. Having had little schooling their geography knowledge was patchy, but what they didn't know they made up. If it was to a particularly strange place the ships were going, even Rosa laughed. After a while they were joined by a boy called Matro, whose father was a fisherman, and he promised they could one day go out on their boat.

Christmas came and went, and so did Isabel's fourteenth birthday. Still, there was no word about papá or his whereabouts. The war seemed to go on and on with no end in sight, and there was never even a suggestion of them going back home.

Then, one day, as they were playing in the park by the harbour, the church bells started to ring. The sound, which had been so familiar to Isabel back home in their village, a part of her everyday life, now filled her with dread. They generally had about a minute, sometimes less, to find shelter before the fascist planes started dropping bombs. She could see nine or ten planes approaching from the west, and all around them people were running and shouting.

One old lady shouted at the children to run for cover before she disappeared down an alleyway.

'Come with me. I know where to go.' Matro ran ahead. They ducked under a fallen streetlight at the far end of the park, running towards the bullring.

Behind them, at the far end of town, explosions could be heard. Isabel turned look, hoping they wouldn't come all the way over to where they stood. Columns of smoke rose from the fires that ran in a line below the five planes, now almost right above. For some reason she couldn't move, couldn't tear her eyes away from the planes that were now too close.

'Isabel, come on.' Luis pulled at her dress and broke the spell. She started running and they almost threw themselves into the small cottage that was Matro's home. As soon as Matro slammed the door shut, the world outside exploded. The house shook with the impact of the explosion, taking Isabel's breath away. She struggled to breathe as dust filled the room. Between coughs she called out for Luis, but the ringing in her ears drowned out any response there might have been. She had to get out, to get some air. The unfamiliar house was dark, and she had no idea how to find the door from which they'd just come in. Then another explosion brought the roof down and everything went black.

She was warm and snug and comfortable where she lay. Isabel slowly opened her eyes. The room she was in felt familiar, yet she couldn't place it. It wasn't home. A wave of nausea came over her when she turned to take a better look around.

'Isabel, you're awake.' Luis came running in and threw his arms around her. 'I was so scared. I thought you were dead.'

In a flash it all came back: the planes and the dust. She tried to sit up, but a pain in the back of her head made her lie down again. 'The raid!' She said, her voice croaky. 'Are you all right?'

'Yes. Rosa is all right, too. They took Matro to the hospital because the glass from the window cut his face. He's going to be fine, though. So they say, anyway.'

'Poor Matro.' She closed her eyes, trying to stop the throbbing pain.

The door opened, and without opening her eyes Isabel could tell from the footsteps it was mamá.

'I thought I heard voices. How are you feeling?' She stroked Isabel's hair from her face.

'My head hurts.'

'You were very lucky. That was a big beam that hit you. You'll have to stay in bed for now.'

'Have you found papá?'

'No, but I will tell you straight away when I do. Now, you must rest.'

Isabel nodded slowly before again closing her eyes. She heard mamá take Luis out of the room and shut the door, then went back to sleep.

After two full days of bombardment there was a general evacuation order. Isabel—who was now walking around the house and feeling better—Luis, and mamá once again packed their bags. The fascists were marching closer and closer, approaching Málaga from the west and from the north, causing the city to panic. Taken by surprise and with no real weapons to defend the city, the commander, Colonel Villalba, feared it would be surrounded and the whole population punished in the same way as Talavera and Badajoz. There, Franco and his army had done exactly as they promised: indiscriminate death and destruction of anyone and anything even slightly connected to the Republic. The only thing Colonel Villalba could do was to order the evacuation of all civilians.

Señora Araya called him a coward and cursed the government for not sending help. Yet she insisted she would still leave the city with them to make sure Luis and Isabel weren't too much trouble for their mamá, who was now heavily pregnant. Irena and Rosa had left the house after the first bombing, when Irena had come back to the house drunk and argumentative. Señora Araya had told her to leave, but said she regretted it now as they hadn't been seen since. As she felt she needed to try and find them, it was decided she would leave Málaga the following day and catch up with them on the only road out of the city that was still open.

Isabel's head felt better, but she worried. How would papá find them now?

Even so, on a bleak day in early February, they left the house in Málaga that had started to feel like their home away from home and started their walk towards yet another new city: Almería.

~ 5 ~

Andalucía, Spain
February 2003

A cold February wind followed them as they walked around the excavation area and Gil explained what was what. The documentary team asked questions, and Gil or Mapi tried to answer. They were all questions the two had answered many times before.

By the side of the trenches, in places where they had found remains or other items of interest, lay numbered cardboard boxes. Their contents were meticulously recorded, and the boxes were kept in a neat and orderly fashion. It was never known when one item, meaningless at the time it was uncovered, would be the factor that proved the identity of somebody's lost relative.

So far, the crew had found five bodies, but none of them had a crushed toe like Mapi's grandfather, José. Her other grandfather, Enrique, had no known distinguishing features so they'd have to rely on the DNA sample she'd provided for his identification. There were, according to the villagers, supposed to be six bodies at this particular site.

After much questioning, they'd learned that the men in this grave had been caught and arrested a couple of days after a nearby battle. The woman who had let them sleep in her barn had gone to find a soldier and told them where they were hiding. After their arrest, they were brought to the village and kept under lock and key. A few days later they were loaded onto a truck and driven away.

Part of Mapi wanted to find José's body. They knew he'd died somewhere in the area and finding him would bring her mamá closure. Another part of her wished it was a big mistake, that he'd made it out of Spain and had lived out his days somewhere else. Like so many other Republican soldiers, perhaps he had helped he resistance in France during the Second World War. But the way her mamá had always talked about him made Mapi certain the first theory would be true. José Mosca would have at some point returned to the village, and to his family, if he'd survived. This was where legend had it he had been killed. Even though her DNA had been taken to match to the bodies once they had found all of them, it could still take up to a month to find out the results.

The crew were filming the area and asking Gil questions. Mapi would talk to them again about her personal side in a couple days' time. They were staying at a fancy golf hotel, and she assumed they wanted to string out their stay as long as they could. The wait suited her as she had to drive to Alicante to pick up her uncle and, if he was sober enough, bring him back for her mamá's surprise eightieth birthday party.

As she looked around, Mapi wondered again why it meant so much to her to have this recorded and broadcast to the world outside Spain. There had been much coverage about stolen babies during the Franco years, yet still the children of mothers deemed unsuitable were missing, the paperwork of their adoptions missing. Why would this be any different? Would the recognition of their pain and silence for the last sixty-four years help, or would the brainwashing of the government still prevail? Mapi couldn't believe there would be any punishment for the criminals who committed these crimes. Most were dead by now anyway, and their memory would not be allowed to be sullied by any criminal judgement of their actions. What did it matter? Most of their victims were dead, too.

Even so, in recent years Spain had acted as a judge in bringing war criminals of other countries to justice—yet they weren't able to deal with their own past. At least with these exhumations the missing could find a home, their relatives finally knowing with certainty where their lost family members were. After more than sixty years, they'd be able to give them a proper burial.

'The burials themselves can sometimes cause issues, and we try to accommodate the families as much as we can.' Mapi overheard Gil speaking to the documentary crew. 'But it's never easy; most of these men weren't religious and they associated the church with the state, the rich landowners, and the industrialists who had taken advantage of them and their families for generations. Now, however, a lot of the families are religious. Conversion was encouraged, if not compulsory, during the Franco years, and many now want their relatives to have a church funeral. There are those who don't want these graves reopened at all; or if they are opened, want the bodies put back as they were found, to lie with their comrades, the cause they fought for being stronger than any other ties. So, you see, it's really rather difficult.'

'Okay, cut there,' Peter said, holding his hand out to Gil. 'Thank you very much for your time. I'm sure we'll see you again as we follow the progress of locating Mapi's grandparents.'

The documentary team set off towards their hotel to do whatever it was they wanted to do, and Gil went back to the dig. Mapi left the site and walked back home to clean up her mamá's front door. Then she would set off for Alicante to pick up Uncle Luis.

***

There was a knock, and Isabel toyed with the idea of not opening the front door. Mapi had a key, and she didn't want to meet anybody else today. Still, she walked through the hallway and turned the lock. Outside stood Señora Encarnita Sanchez Salazar, looking very serious.

'Isabel, what has happened here?' She took a step back and looked at the wall. Confused, Isabel stepped out onto the street to see what she was talking about.

There it was. It had started. It was there for everybody to see, and for them to either pity her or despise her. *Rojo*. So many years of silence and obeying the rules, and now it had started again. What would be next? Stones thrown through her windows? Glares and comments as she walked down to the shops? Isabel hadn't wanted it then and she didn't need it now.

But she refused to let Encarnita see how the word affected her, so she shook her head and ushered her indoors.

'Some bored children. I'll wash it off later,' she said, as if it didn't really matter. She busied herself making coffee.

Encarnita was part of *them*, part of the village's right-wing circle. Well, that's to say her husband was and she, being the good wife, supported him like she'd supported her father before. Isabel knew her neighbour's father had been a landowner, overseeing the land her own papá, and generations before him, had worked. If Isabel had only known about the graffiti beforehand, she could have washed it off before anyone saw it, or she could have asked Mapi to paint it over.

'Isabel, I'll send Manuel over to help with that nastiness outside. You can't do it on your own.'

Manuel was her thug of a grandson, and Isabel was sure it was he who had probably done it in the first place.

'No, no. I couldn't ask you to do that. My Mapi will do it when she gets back.'

Encarnita tapped her fingers on the table before helping herself to a biscuit. 'I think she is the problem, Isabel. Don't get me wrong, I think she's a wonderful woman and a credit to you, but she has stirred up the village. Some things are just better left the way they are. Young ones don't understand what we went through, and it must never be repeated.'

Isabel agreed because it was easier. She was too old now to get involved.

'Everything that happened back then is best left where it is.' Encarnita repeated.

For a moment Isabel thought that maybe things weren't best forgotten about. Maybe, to put everything to sleep, it first had to be woken up and dealt with, or it would always keep haunting them. The thing was that Isabel was not the person to do it; she never had been. But maybe Mapi was.

'And those British television people, why are they here? What has it got to do with them? They like to judge the world, don't they? So, Isabel, have you spoken to them?'

There we go, Isabel thought, *that's the reason you're here.* Señora Encarnita wanted to know if Mapi had told anybody what her grandparents, and all the rest of them, had done during the Franco years. For a second, Isabel thought she might lie and say she'd spoken to them at length and told them everything: that the history of Encarnita's family and friends would be broadcast to the world. They might not be judged in Spain, but, if they only knew, they would be judged by the world. *Well, at least until something juicier comes along.*

'I'm too old to talk to anybody,' Isabel said instead, 'and what would I say? There is nothing to tell, is there?'

Encarnita gave a patronising smile and took Isabel's hand. 'No, there isn't. Please tell Mapi that, too.' She paused. 'So, how are you finding life in the village? It must be nearly a year now since you moved here. It's a lot easier, isn't it? No more long trips just to get to the shops, and the church is so much closer. We have lots of help to give you if needed.'

'Well, everybody has been really friendly and helpful,' Isabel replied. She didn't say how she'd never wanted to leave the farmhouse, with all the good memories of her life etched into its stone walls. It was still the place she thought of as home, but now someone else was turning it into a holiday house.

She could tell Encarnita wasn't quite sure how to take the comment but seemed to decide to interpret it as friendly. She stood up. 'I'll ask Manuel to paint over that filth. He'll do it before the weekend, I'm sure.'

Isabel walked her to the front door. 'Please don't trouble him. I'm sure he's busy with other things.' She just wanted the awful woman to go, and she didn't want her grandson near her house again.

'Well, goodbye for now. I'll see you at....' She smiled. 'Oops, I nearly spoiled the surprise.'

Isabel nodded, not having heard the last sentence. She resisted the urge to slam the door shut. She was angry now and could feel the blood rushing through her head as she sat down on the sofa.

She had already told her story, spending years after her husband's death writing it all down. Word by word she'd recorded it all for Mapi, so her daughter would know her properly and so she would know all the things Isabel couldn't bring herself to say out loud. Those long days and nights spent on her own up at the farmhouse before she was made to move into the village had been put to good use. Every little thing she could remember, Isabel had written down—even the parade and what had happened after. She'd denied it to herself for so long that Isabel almost wasn't sure it had happened at all. Yet she only had to look at the scars on her arms to know that it had.

Still, she had thought about burning what she'd written quite a few times. Why bring up the past when it was so grim? The only answer she could think of was that everybody deserves justice, and if they can't have that, then they at least deserve to be heard.

Isabel walked into the bedroom and opened her bedside table drawer. In there, together with the photograph and other bits of her life, lay a black notebook with a label glued to the front. 'To Mapi, our history,' it read.

She put the photograph of her father next to the letter inside the notebook. Mapi didn't think she knew about the surprise party, but she did, and Isabel had decided she would give her the notebook then. It contained many things, things Isabel should have told her daughter about many years ago, but hadn't. She hoped Mapi would be able to forgive her.

~ 6 ~

**Andalucía, Spain
February 1937**

Thousands of Spanish civilians, all fleeing their homes, moved slowly east, away from a burning Málaga—of which the fascists were now in control. The road they walked twisted between the mountains on their left and the Mediterranean on their right, and the line of refugees stretched out in front of and behind of Isabel as far as her eyes could see. People carried their possessions on their backs, or piled up on carts pulled and pushed by whole households. Some were lucky enough to have a car or a truck, but the road wasn't wide enough for them to pass so they were stuck with everybody else. Behind them, chasing them, trying to catch them, were the fascists—a knowledge that struck fear into every heart.

Isabel and Luis had to take turns carrying mamá's bag because she couldn't handle the weight with that of their baby brother or sister. Isabel worried about her silence, always an indication something was wrong. If she shouted, screamed, or gesticulated wildly it meant she was fine and their world was as it should be. Now, she walked without saying a word, putting one foot in front of the other again and again, her thoughts somewhere else.

'There are ships out there.' Luis pointed towards the sea, where three large grey warships had appeared on the horizon. 'I'd like to go on one of those.' He kicked a stone in front of him, suddenly sour. 'I'm thirsty. Is there any water somewhere, mamá?'

'You know there isn't. She told you earlier.' Isabel answered for her.

'It's strange that all that water is just there,' he said, looking at the sea stretching out to their right, 'so close I could run into it, but there's nothing to drink. Matro said you can't drink sea water because it's salty, but olives are salty and we eat them.' Luis kept on talking even though Isabel or mamá rarely gave a response. 'Where do you think Matro is? If he came out of hospital he could be anywhere, maybe even here.' He looked at the other refugees crowding the road all around them. There were so many it was impossible to move any faster or slower. Just in front was a horse and cart, fully loaded with whatever the owners could bring; an old woman sat on top. Her face was lined with years of work and sunshine, and from time to time they could hear her shouting orders to her daughter-in-law below.

Today, their second day on the road, the sun shone upon the sea as if nothing was wrong in the world. Isabel wanted to go back home to La Quida and sit on the barrels and look out over the mountain. If they could only go back to the way it was, she wouldn't even complain about doing chores or having to go to school. They hadn't done anything wrong, so why did the soldiers want to kill them? They couldn't kill everybody just because they had a different opinion. She had tried to convince mamá they should walk in the opposite direction, back to their little house, but it was to no avail. Instead, they trudged slowly along while rumours of fascists shooting or beheading anybody they caught travelled up and down the line of refugees. When Isabel got too tired, or her feet hurt too much, she pictured the fascists catching up with them, imagining how they would be killed.

Mamá, heavily pregnant with their brother or sister, struggled with every step. Her face was now pale and gleamed with sweat that hadn't been there hours before, forcing them to take rests more frequently. Other women asked if she was all right, and to let them know if she needed help when the time came. Isabel worried because mamá had become terribly quiet, as if every ounce of energy she had was put into moving forwards. She thought about asking the old woman on the cart if she'd consider swapping places with mamá, for just a little while, but she was too scared. The old woman would sometimes glare at her when Isabel looked to ask, and she would quickly return her gaze to the road.

'Don't you think it's strange that we can't drink it, Isabel? It's right there.' Luis nudged her. 'Look.'

'Oh, for God's sake, Luis, I know it's there. Go and drink it if you want.'

'We'd be sick if we drank it, but I don't know why. I don't think it's the salt, because as I said, olives are salty, and they don't kill us.'

'Olives aren't salty to start with, we add the salt to store them. You know that.'

'Mamá, shall I find us some water?

'That would be good, darling.' Even mamá's voice was tired.

'If you could find some water to drink you would be a miracle worker. Or a thief,' Isabel said. 'And we don't like either of those.'

'You're very mean.'

'Yes, I am. Why don't you go and talk to those boys up there?' She pointed at some boys further up the road Luis had made friends with the previous night while they briefly rested.

He glanced with worry at mamá. 'Don't stop anywhere without telling me,' he said before running up ahead.

Luis had just disappeared from Isabel's view when the droning sound of airplanes reached her from the coast. The noise got louder and louder. She grew cold with fear and very quickly the refugees realised what they planned to do—but there was nowhere to run. The road was cut into the hillside of the high Sierra Nevada Mountains; on the other side was the unforgiving Mediterranean Sea.

The machine guns on the front plane started shooting.

Mamá grabbed Isabel's hand, pulling her out of the way as the strafing came closer. People were screaming and pushing from every side, but mamá pulled her away and put her arms around her shoulders. Isabel buried her face in her mamá's shawl and felt her arms protect her like a magic cape. People all around them were screaming, either from pain or terror. Her body tense, Isabel kept her eyes closed and breathed in mamá's comforting scent.

During a lull in the gunfire, when the planes flew further along the road, mamá managed to get to her feet so Isabel followed, still holding tightly to her hand.

'Where is my son?' She shouted his name. 'Luis!'

Isabel joined in, but in the chaos their voices couldn't be heard.

A flash from one of the boats on the horizon caught Isabel's eye and a sudden whining noise ended in an explosion. The bomb landed further down the road and sent a cloud of dust their way. The whining sound was heard again.

With shaking hands they climbed up a steep hillside, mamá shouting for Luis as a shell landed where they'd been just a few minutes earlier. Coughing on the dust they managed to get halfway up the mountain, where Isabel found a dense bush that offered no protection if they were seen or if a shell landed too close, but it was the only place they had time to find; others below weren't so lucky.

Isabel's heart beat hard and she shut her eyes tight, putting her fingers in her ears to block the explosions and the screams as the planes returned. When the shelling from the ships sent down showers of dry earth and stones, Isabel tried to remember La Quida: the crossroads where she used to meet papá, the warm stone by the kitchen window, even the school, but it was no use. Every time she thought she could see it in front of her, a shell or a row of bullets hit the mountain and instantly she was back in their nightmare. It was then she realised mamá was lying down on the red earth just behind her.

Her eyes were closed, her face patchy with sweat and mud

'Is the baby coming?' Isabel asked.

Mamá nodded. 'We have to find Luis. I don't know if I have the strength for this.'

With a hollow sound, a blast of bullets hit the base of the bush, but then the sound of the planes' engines died away. For a brief moment an eerie calm spread over the road and the hillside. Time stood still while the survivors looked around in shock at the devastation. Then mamá's screams started, tearing a hole in Isabel's soul.

'Mamá, how can I help?' She was frantic. 'Tell me what to do.' Isabel wiped the wet mud from mamá's face, wishing they'd stayed in Málaga. Her mouth was dry with fear and she wanted to cry, but she had to be strong. She knew she had to get mamá help but was scared to leave her on her own. Isabel could see no other option. 'The planes seem to have gone now, mamá. I'll go and fetch someone to help.'

Mamá nodded weakly. 'And find your brother,' she whispered.

When Isabel crawled out from their hiding place behind the bush, she couldn't stop the tears, through which she saw the devastation below. Dead or injured people lay on the road or at its side, or were being carried away by survivors. She wondered briefly if the beam that had hit her head the previous week had sent her mad. How could a place like this exist? However, it wasn't a trick being played by her mind, and with tears streaming down her dusty face she slid down the hillside.

On the road survivors hurried past to try and find a safer place—they all knew the planes and ships would return. All around were shouts of anger and cries of pain from the injured. Tears wet the faces of those people still alive. She couldn't see her brother anywhere, or either of the two women who had offered to help mamá earlier.

Isabel pulled on the sleeve of one woman standing by the roadside, looking out over the devastation.

'Señora, my mamá needs help. She's giving birth and she's not well.'

The woman looked down on her with glazed eyes and shook her head. 'Can't you see all this? Your mamá should be able to give birth on her own. She's got you to help.'

Then, as if in a trance, the woman turned around and started walking away.

The sun was setting, and Isabel was in a state of panic. She had to find someone to help. Then she heard the whistle of incoming shells. Once again, the sound filled the air, and the planes approached in the distance.

The shell exploded high on the hillside, just below her mamá. As fast as she could, Isabel turned around and crawled back up through the dust. The shell had made a dent in the earth below, but their hiding place was still safe. She found mamá still on her back, a trickle of blood moving along the dry mud.

'Mamá.' Isabel touched her face. 'I couldn't find anybody, but I'll help you. What do I do?'

Mamá opened her eyes. 'You have to look after the baby, Ratoncito.'

'The baby?' She looked around in confusion before seeing it by mamá's side. He'd been sprayed with earth from the bomb, but his face was clear and his eyes were blinking.

When she heard the next whistle, Isabel covered her head with her arms and put herself protectively over the baby. 'I've got him, mamá,' she whispered.

It was dark when the planes finally left. Isabel spat on a corner of her skirt and cleaned the baby as best she could. He was so little.

'They seem to have gone quiet again. Shall I go and see if I can find Luis?' Mamá's eyes remained closed and a feeling of dread settled over her. 'Mamá? Wake up. Wake up.'

Her eyes flickered open and tried to focus on her daughter. 'I am so sorry, Isabel. You must find Luis and papá. Promise me.'

Isabel nodded because there was nothing else she could do. Mamá lay dying in front of her and she couldn't help. 'I promise,' she said, lying down beside her. Her face next to mamá's she breathed in her scent, her new brother between them. 'Don't leave me,' she whispered.

Isabel heard the last breath her mamá took, her last heartbeat, before she was left alone on this road of death.

After a while, with a strange detachment to the world, Isabel put her hand in her mamá's pocket and took out the photo of papá. She sat up and put it in her pocket. She knew she had to keep the baby warm, so she unwrapped the scarf from her mamá's shoulders and used it to cover the baby. It smelled like mamá.

Isabel picked the baby up and, as if all this was happening to somebody else, slowly climbed down the mountain. mamá needed to be buried, but she first had to find Luis. Suddenly, she was the one responsible for the three of them, but she couldn't think about that right now. They just needed to get away from the guns and the shells and this road.

The baby was heavier than she thought he'd be, and Isabel's thin arms ached even as she reached the road. In the moonlight that flitted in and out between clouds she saw a scene that would stay with her forever. There were even more dead bodies strewn across the road and the hillside.

Hundreds and hundreds of mothers, fathers, brothers, and sisters lay there, all lifeless and abandoned by their families who were now moving as fast as they could up the road where there might be some shelter from further attacks.

With the baby in her arms Isabel scanned the bodies, shouting her brother's name in case he was still hiding. There was no reply. She asked people walking past if they'd seen Luis, if they'd help bury her mamá. Some were sympathetic, and some weren't, but all of them said no or simply ignored her.

When the darkness seeped into her, and the only light was the moon shimmering off the sea, Isabel turned around and started walking back towards her home, towards La Quida.

Progress was slow because she had to carry the baby and take regular breaks. He needed food, but she had nothing to give. She'd had nothing to eat or drink herself for almost two days, and from time to time Isabel fought off the faintness that came from lack of water and hope. The only thing that kept her going was the thought of being back on the farm. Back in the beautiful mountains that was their home. She'd tell her aunt and her neighbours what had happened, and they would find mamá and bury her properly in the village where she belonged. Luis would think the same thing and would also be walking back home, somewhere along the road in front of her.

A tired stream of Republicans from Málaga and beyond still struggled along the road towards Almería, all wanting to get as much distance between themselves and the city as they could. But she was the only one walking in the opposite direction.

Isabel caught the odd look from those on the roadside resting their blistered feet. They were too wrapped up in their own grief to care much about anybody else's, so she continued walking against the flow. The night air was chilly as she walked numbly back up the road they'd come down only that morning, when they'd all still been together.

Gentle ocean waves washed up over the stones on the shore, trying to clean the air of the screams of terror that had filled it that afternoon. Eerily, the souls of the dead hovered above their bodies, urging their families, comrades, and neighbours to run far away. If there was such a thing as hell, this must be the road leading to it. As far as Isabel could see in the moonlight, hundreds of dead bodies lined the roadside, having been moved off the road. If she allowed herself to think about what had happened that day, she would have gone mad. Why would anybody do this?

Isabel tried to stop thinking and concentrate on the road ahead, but she didn't know where she was going. She might not be able to cross through the centre of Málaga, so it would be best to keep to the outside roads. When she came to a crossroad, she'd know which one to take. She'd follow the road via the forests she'd seen on their journey to Málaga last October.

'Isabel? Is that you?'

She recognised the voice that called after her, but couldn't place it, and in the dark, she couldn't see who spoke. 'Who's there?'

From the other side of the road Señora Araya emerged, and Isabel felt she could cry with relief.

'It's me, Señora Araya. Where's your mamá?' She looked at the wrapped parcel in Isabel's arms. 'Is she all right?'

Isabel shook her head. She didn't move as the Señora took the baby from her and looked at him a moment before putting her hand on his neck. Then she turned her attention back to Isabel.

'Did you know the baby is dead, Isabel?'

Again, Isabel shook her head.

'Come.' Señora Araya indicated for Isabel to follow, and a short bit down the road they stopped. The moon showed a small hole in the ground where a shell had landed earlier. The Señora covered the baby's body fully in the shawl and put him gently down. It was so dark that he blended into the dry mud even before the Señora had covered him with earth.

'Does he have a name?'

'José, like my father.'

'Okay.' She put three stones on top of the grave, so they could find it again. 'Do you want to say a prayer?'

'No. Papá says we don't do that now.'

'Well, we can do it properly when all this madness has settled down. Although I'm not sure Spain will ever recover.'

They walked back to where Señora Araya had first spotted Isabel.

'Come sit with us. Irena is here, too. She's sleeping for an hour or so until we move again.' They sat down by the side of the road and the Señora took her hand. 'Isabel, tell me what happened.'

At first Isabel shook her head, but the Señora somehow coaxed it all out. As she told her what had happened she couldn't stop her right foot from tapping the mud. When she finished Señora Araya squeezed her hand.

'We lost Rosa in a bomb raid before we left.' She sighed. 'It's all so terribly sad, but tomorrow we can say a proper goodbye to your mamá and somewhere we'll find your brother.'

'I'm going back home.'

'No, you're not. Look what they've done here. What do you think is left of your friends and neighbours?' The Señora spoke harshly, not remembering she was talking to a thirteen-year-old girl who had just lost her family. 'Besides, what about Luis? He's all on his own and you're all he has.'

Isabel couldn't take it all in and just looked at the ground, her mind blank. She didn't care if they killed her now.

The Señora shook her by the shoulders to get her attention. 'Did you hear what I just said? Do you think your mamá would have wanted you to abandon your brother?'

I already have, Isabel thought, glancing in the direction of José's grave.

'I can't make you do anything, Isabel. If you want to walk back to your home, I can't stop you.'

Isabel took a deep breath. She knew Señora Araya was right: she had to find Luis. If he was still alive, that was.

'I'm going to wake Irena.' The Señora stood up. 'Then we'll get away from this road of the dead.'

***

They walked for four nights, hiding wherever they could during the daylight hours when the planes returned with their machine guns, the ships with their shells. Whenever they found somewhere to rest and sleep, Isabel closed her eyes and images of mamá and the dead bodies that covered the road appeared behind her lids. On the odd occasion she fell asleep she woke covered in a cold sweat and crying for mamá. Every day they hoped there would be a break in the killing and the government's forces would come to their rescue, but they didn't. It was as if the Republic had washed their hands of them and left them to die.

They walked at the back of the column that snaked its way north-wards and so had to keep moving as fast as they could to avoid capture by the Nationalists who chased them by tank, by car, and by foot to return as many as they could to Málaga. What fate awaited the ones they caught was not something anybody wanted to dwell upon.

The villages on the route to Almería had been saturated with refugees, and many of the locals kept their front doors closed and refused to help as it looked increasingly likely the Nationalists would take their village too. They probably couldn't have helped much anyway, as food and water were scarce and thousands of refugees would have passed through before Isabel, the Señora, and Irena trudged along their main roads in silence.

For the four days it took them to reach the outskirts of Almería they'd only drank one cup of water each, and their only sustenance had been a couple of sugar canes Señora Araya had bought with the last of her money.

When they arrived in the city there was nowhere to stay. The streets swelled with refugees and the port was so full they couldn't even find anywhere to sit down.

'Will they help us here?' Isabel asked, her voice hoarse from lack of water as they joined the queue outside a building the Señora said helped to evacuate refugees.

'How can they? Look around you. Everyone here needs help. There's too many.' Irena's voice, also raspy from lack of water, was short with irritation.

'What else do you suggest we do?' The Señora looked sternly at Irena. 'Sit down on the pavement and wait to die?'

Irena, not having a better idea nor the energy to think of one, stayed quiet.

'What about Luis? They might know where he is,' Isabel said quietly, hoping only the Señora could hear. Irena's stinging comments had been directed at the two of them as they had been delayed by Isabel's insistence they bury mamá before moving along. It had proved impossible, and in the end, they placed, by her body, a flower from a nearby bush and moved on. They hadn't really had any other choice; they had to move forward to avoid capture and to find a better hiding place for the morning. Isabel knew all this, but when she closed her eyes she could still see her mamá, cold and alone.

'If Luis came here he'll be looked after somewhere, I'm sure,' the Señora said.

That's when a large woman, dressed in black and wearing a Republican badge, came out of the building to address the waiting refugees. She took up a position at the front of the queue and spoke in a roar.

'If you require housing and food there is nothing we can do for you here. I am sorry, but you will have to make do for the time being. There is assistance on the way, but until then we have nothing to give you.' The statement was brief, and shouts of anger could be heard from those in the queue.

Isabel ran up to the woman before she had a chance to go back inside. 'My brother went missing on the way here. Do you know where we can find him? Please.'

'How old is he?'

'He's only seven, Señora.'

'Well, there are two orphanages here in Almería. He may well be there. Come inside.'

The lady led the way through a large hall filled with people and walked up some stairs into a small office that looked like it used to be a cleaning cupboard. 'Can any of you read?'

Señora Araya spoke up. 'I can.' She took the piece of paper on which the lady had written the addresses of the orphanages. 'Is there anywhere in this town where we can get some food and water?'

'I'm afraid not. Almería is a small city with only 50,000 citizens, and the flood of refugees from Málaga is 40,000 to 50,000. So, you see, we have doubled in size over just a few days.' She picked up her bag from the floor and took out two dry oranges. 'Here, have these. The girl can have a glass of milk before you leave.' She shook her head. 'I'm so sorry for what you've been through.'

Too hungry to allow the pride that normally would have made them decline the offer, the Señora put the two oranges in her pocket.

'Thank you. These are bad times we live in.'

The lady nodded. 'They are indeed.'

After Isabel had drunk the milk that would normally have made her stomach turn and they had shared the oranges, they walked towards the first orphanage's address.

'We should leave this town,' Irena said. 'If we go into the mountains we can pick our food and wait for our army.'

'You wouldn't know what to pick, or how to cook it,' the Señora replied.

'She would, though.' Irena nodded towards Isabel. 'You know how to forage for food and stuff, don't you? Being from the countryside.'

'I can find some things. It's not season yet though,' Isabel responded quietly.

'If we had a gun we could shoot some animals and have meat, too,' Irena continued.

'God help us if you ever had a gun,' Señora Araya said before looking up at a ramshackle townhouse. 'Well, here we are.'

A short thin woman with glasses opened the door. Behind her they could see lots of children lacking the energy and life they should have. Dressed in rags and with dirty faces they glanced at the visitors. But the woman noticed only Isabel, and before they had a chance to speak, she said very brusquely, 'No. We have no more room here. You have to go to the committee for—'

'No, no. We're just looking for someone,' the Señora interrupted. 'His name is Luis and he's seven years old. He went missing on the road from Málaga.' She searched the faces of the children she could see through the door. 'Do you know if he's been taken here?'

The surly woman sighed. 'He might have. Over the last few days we've had at least two hundred children arrive, their parents either dead or missing.' She opened the door wide. 'Come in and have a look if you like.'

They went inside and walked through the misery that lived there. The boys and the girls, whose lives hadn't deserved such a bad start, looked at them in silence as they walked past, but nowhere could they find Luis. They thanked the woman and started walking to the next orphanage.

'What do we do if he's not there?' Isabel asked.

'Don't worry, we'll find him somewhere....'

A few streets down the church bells started ringing and they looked at each other in dismay.

'Oh, no,' whispered the Señora just before the sound of the planes for a brief second sucked all other senses away. Then the bombs started falling and they had no idea where to hide. In the end, they sat huddled together on the pavement by a large townhouse and hoped they would be all right. The ground shook as bomb after bomb was dropped. The air quickly filled with acrid smoke from the burning buildings, and with dust from the houses that collapsed under impact.

The exhaustion and trauma of the last few days, the attacks on the road, and now this bombing of the city where they sat unprotected, finally took its toll on Isabel. The panic that filled her at the thought of what was happening, the fact she was all alone in the world, sent loud screams of terror from her mouth. Her vision had gone blurry and she hid her face in her dress, but she couldn't stop screaming.

Even when she felt the Señora's arms around her, holding her tight, she couldn't stop. Isabel screamed until her voice wouldn't function anymore. The Señora continued holding her, and when the bombs stopped and the planes went back to wherever they'd come, the screams echoing down the street did not come from Isabel.

From all over came shrieks of grief from mothers whose children were injured or dead, and loud curses from both militia and injured civilians. The three of them rose from where they sat, and Isabel's legs felt like jelly. Yet not a word about her outburst was mentioned, and they walked arm in arm through the orange glow of the burning city towards the next orphanage. They acted as if this last raid had never happened; it was almost as though they had adapted to a life in which this was normal.

Isabel had calmed down and walked silently along the two ladies who were the only friends she now had in this world. Five months ago they had been strangers, but now they shared every last minute of their lives together. She held on tightly to Señora Araya's arm as they pushed through crowds of desolate refugees: past the elderly who should have been cared for by their families and not driven from their homes, past those starved and terrorised by war, past hundreds of people who had done nothing wrong apart from wanting a fair wage and a decent life. None of them deserved this. None.

The flames coming from the second orphanage could be seen from the end of the road. Plumes of smoke reached for the dark sky, and on the street outside stood the surviving children watching it burn.

The milk and the orange had done nothing to soften Isabel's hunger; in fact, they had only made it worse. She quietly scoured the face of every boy she saw to make sure she didn't miss Luis. He had to be here. She refused to believe that he was lying dead or injured on the side of that road, with nobody to look after him. They tried to find someone in charge but in the chaos on the street, they couldn't.

'They don't need our help, and it's getting dark. We need to find somewhere to sleep,' the Señora said. 'We can search further tomorrow,' she added, seeing the look on Isabel's face. 'We'll come back tomorrow. Just now they have enough to deal with.'

But as they were about to leave, Isabel heard someone call her name from further down the street.

'Wait. Isabel! Wait for me.' Luis shouted so loudly he could be heard over the roar of the burning building and the clanging of the fire engine. He ran towards them.

'Luis.' Isabel tried to shout, but her voice wouldn't work.

He threw his arms around her and squeezed. 'I thought you'd never find me.' He looked around. 'Where's mamá?'

'Where have you been? How did you get here?' Whether Señora Araya asked to avoid either herself or Isabel having to answer his question she couldn't tell.

'I couldn't find you, and my friends said I couldn't wait for you on the road. I walked here with them, but they took me to the orphanage.' Luis pointed to the burning building.

'They said this town was too full of people, so they walked somewhere else. I can't remember where. They said to wait here for you.'

'And you're all right? No injuries?'

Luis shook his head and turned his attention back to Isabel, smiling. 'Where's mamá, Isabel?' His little face looked up at that of his big sister whose eyes had started to water. In her throat was a large lump that threatened to turn into vomit. She couldn't bring herself to tell him.

'Irena, go over there and tell someone we're taking Luis with us, and bring Isabel with you. We don't want them to think they've lost him.' The Señora was firm in her instructions. 'Quickly now.'

Relived they had found Luis, and relieved Señora Araya had taken charge of the situation, Isabel only somewhat reluctantly followed Irena.

They walked over to one of the women who had appeared outside the burning orphanage and told her who they were, that Luis would go with them. She didn't like the idea of letting one of the children go without the relevant paperwork, but there were so many she was pleased one had found some family.

'Please get the paperwork to me tomorrow or the day after. It will all be fine,' she said before turning her attention back to the other children.

Isabel didn't want to go back to where her brother was standing with Señora Araya. She knew she'd have told Luis what had happened, and she was scared she wouldn't be able to cope with his grief as well as her own.

How could she tell him that their mamá's body lay barely covered with mud behind a rosemary bush because they hadn't had time to bury her properly? How his new brother had died and was lying underneath some stones by the side of the road, all alone and far away from his mamá? That, until they found papá, it was only the two of them left?

Yet when they reached the Señora and Luis they weren't met by a crying boy, but rather one who looked a little older as he filed the death of his mamá amongst the other atrocities he'd seen in the last few weeks to be dealt with later. Isabel took his hand and squeezed it tightly. The four walked away from the still-burning fires.

Señora Araya managed to buy them each a bowl of soup from a local man who grudgingly accepted her wedding ring as payment. It was rather watery, but hot with bits of rice and vegetables, and tasted as good as the best meal gold could buy. After, they slept in the same place as most other refugees: along the streets leading down to the harbour. Isabel closed her eyes and told Luis one of the old stories from home. Her arms were wrapped around him and his head rested on her shoulder. If she hadn't met the Señora on that road he would have been left at the orphanage forever, and she would never have known.

The pavement was cold and hard on her back, but she didn't want to move as she might wake Luis, who had fallen asleep. Around them the city continued to burn, and its orange glow lit up the dark night sky. Her brother's even breathing made Isabel sleepy, and reluctantly she let her eyelids shut.

At dawn the following morning she woke with aches and pains from sleeping on the hard pavement. She shivered from the cold as she sat up. Around them displaced people were arriving or leaving, or just wandering around trying to find somewhere warm to spend a few hours.

Next to her, Luis was still asleep. He'd woken from bad dreams in the night, but she'd put her arms around him and he'd gone back to sleep. Just the fact they were together made everything a little easier. Just having her brother next to her, someone from the good life they'd had before the war, eased a little of her own pain. She'd look after him now until they found papá; he would make everything right again.

'Good morning,' the Señora said sleepily. 'I can't possibly sleep like this another night. My back is aching.' She sat up next to Isabel and looked around. 'Where's Irena?'

'I don't know.' Isabel secretly hoped she'd gone forever. She was mean, and they would be better off without her.

'How is your brother?'

'He's all right, I think. He woke up in the night but went back to sleep.'

'Poor boy. He has been very brave.'

'We need to find our papá now, Señora.'

The Señora smiled reassuringly. 'Of course you do. We'll find him, but it may take a little time.' Her eyes focused on something further down the road. 'Here comes Irena. She seems to be in a hurry.'

'Why is she so mean?' Isabel asked as she turned her head and watched as she hurried towards them.

'She's had a hard life. Let's not judge her for that.'

Irena arrived, bent down, and whispered, 'Food's arrived. We must hurry if we're to get any.'

'Luis, wake up.' Isabel lightly shook her brother's shoulder and he opened his eyes. She could see he'd forgotten, for just that moment, where they were and what had happened.

With a sleepy and disoriented Luis, they scrambled to their feet and followed Irena.

News of the food distribution had reached most by the time they got there, and people appeared from various streets, rushing towards the main square.

Soldiers with old and outdated rifles slung over their shoulders organised queues in an almost orderly fashion. If Irena hadn't alerted them, they would be queuing along the surrounding streets, as hundreds were, instead of being inside the square.

There was a piece of bread, a small bag of rice, and one orange per person. They would have to find someone to cook the rice, or trade it for something else. Sitting by the harbour they ate some of the bread but kept the fruit for later. Before them the sea shimmered in the weak sunshine and, away from the crowds of refugees and the burnt buildings, it could have been a normal day.

But it wasn't a normal day. Isabel's eyes kept returning to the skies down the coast, searching for planes; her ears alert for the sound of shells from one of the big ships, her right foot tapping the cobbles while she finished her bread. She saw the Señora and Irena glance in the direction of Málaga from time to time, no doubt keeping alert for a possible attack. She wished Luis would talk nonsense about seawater and all the other things that had annoyed her before, but he just sat next to her and ate his bread in silence.

'We can't stay here,' the Señora said. 'There are too many refugees and Málaga is too close. I have a cousin in Alicante. Maybe she will let us stay at her house until we find somewhere else.'

'If she's still there,' Irena said.

'Well, we can't stay here. So unless you have another suggestion we should go. It can't be any worse than here.'

'Is it far away?' Isabel asked. 'We have to find papá, and if we go too far away we'll never find him.'

'Wait until all this settles down and then we'll find him for you. He'll be busy fighting the fascists now, anyway. You want him to fight, don't you?'

Isabel hesitated at the Señora's question because she didn't want him to fight at all, but she knew she should say that she did. 'Yes. But I'd like us to be with him.'

'You stay with me and Irena for now, and then we'll see what we can do.' She squeezed Isabel's hand. 'If we're lucky we might be able to find a cart we can ride on.'

'You'd have to be lucky,' Irena said. 'I think everybody in their right mind will try to get out of this town before the fascists arrive.'

The Señora looked at her newly acquired family and smiled. 'There you go. We're agreed. We're going to Alicante.'

~ 7 ~

Alicante, Spain
February 2003

Alicante was chilly and quiet. It had been a long day and Mapi felt exhausted as she drove along the palm-lined seafront. She was later than she'd hoped, but it could have been worse: she might have had to repaint her mother's house to get rid of the graffiti. As it was it had taken her thirty minutes, plus the lunch mamá had made her have, before she'd been able to set off on her secret mission to bring her uncle back to her mamá. It was the best present she could think to give. She'd told her mamá she was going back to Madrid for a meeting but would be back the following day by lunchtime.

The sky was cloudy and cold gusts of wind leapt in from the sea. To avoid driving through the old town she parked at the seafront and walked. She preferred the town like this, not full of holidaymakers, when it was easy to park and get a meal in a restaurant. She didn't visit very often; the only thing for her here was her uncle, and he was drunk more often than not. He'd come to her father's funeral, but that was over ten years ago and he'd left very quickly. His friend, Pepe, with whom he'd lived for—well, she didn't know how long—had come with him. Mapi got the feeling that if it hadn't been for Pepe, Luis wouldn't have gone at all. They'd left before anybody had a chance to talk to him.

Mamá was upset by the rift, but Mapi didn't know its cause. She wasn't even sure they did anymore. Then again, people sometimes drift apart. Live far away from each other for a long period of time and almost everybody will find it difficult to have a conversation. She'd heard so much about Luis as she grew up that one day she decided to contact him and they now spoke regularly on the phone; she tried to visit when she could.

Pepe had died the previous year and left Luis the house. Even though it was rundown and in need of a serious renovation, it gave him somewhere to live. He was seventy-four and he'd worked as a fisherman his whole life, so Mapi knew he should have enough of a pension coming in to cover at least the basic bills.

The cobbled street was quiet, with residential houses and only a few shops and bars frequented by the locals; tourists were instead drawn to the main streets and squares. Her uncle's house was dark, and there was no answer when Mapi knocked. After a few moments she tried to open the door and found it was unlocked.

She called out from the dark hallway. 'Hola, Tío Luis. It's me, Mapi.' It smelled as if nobody had lived there in years, but she knew her uncle hadn't left. He'd at least been there the day before, when she'd spoken to him over the phone. The conversation had been short, and he'd slurred his words, but she'd made him write the time of her arrival down on a piece of paper.

Mapi walked through the hallway and into the kitchen. On the pine table stood two empty bottles of wine and the remnants of a torn loaf, surrounded by crumbs. Light leaked from the ajar fridge door, and she pushed it shut before striding up the stairs. She found Luis on the bathroom floor, out cold. Her lips pressed thin in anger before she filled an empty toothbrush holder with water and threw it over him. He knew how important this was: his sisters', his only sisters', eightieth birthday party. They were getting old and might not get another chance to meet.

The water hit Luis, and his eyes opened wide in confusion. 'What....' He stared, unfocused, at his niece. 'What's happened?'

'You're a liar, that's what. You promised you would stay sober.'

'Ah, I am.' He closed his eyes again. 'Just tired.'

'You normally sleep on the bathroom floor? Come on,' Mapi said, 'get up.'

'Soon, just let me sleep for a few minutes and I'll be....'

Luis had fallen back to sleep. Mapi again filled the toothbrush holder with water and threw it once more over his face. 'Come on,' she said when he opened his eyes. 'We'll have something to eat and a good night's sleep. Tomorrow you're coming with me to your sisters'. I will drag you there if I have to, conscious or not.'

Mapi managed to get Luis downstairs and seated at the kitchen table before he passed out. He sat in a chair, elbows on the table and red, puffed-up face in his hands. His white hair looked as if it needed washing, and judging by the smell, so did the rest of him. She could tell by his even breathing, interrupted only by an occasional cough, that he slept deeply. There was no food in the cupboards so, after pouring a bottle of wine down the sink, she went to the little shop on the corner and bought potatoes, onion, garlic, and a thick cut of bacon. *If that doesn't sober him up, nothing will.* She also picked up some coffee, milk, and bread for toasting in the morning.

The first time Mapi had visited, some years earlier, Luis had been an unfriendly, arrogant shit of a man, not wanting anything to do with her. The wheelchair-bound Pepe had been nicer, and in the end, Luis had got used to her visits and no longer glared whenever she arrived. He would not talk about his history or about his sister, and Mapi wondered how two siblings could grow so far apart. When Pepe had died, she had gone to his funeral, but Isabel had not been invited. In his will, Pepe had left the house to Luis, and Mapi had found a note that he'd written to his friend. In it he said how sorry he was for Luis having given up his life to look after him. Luis just shrugged his shoulders and said, in a moment of soberness, that anybody would have done the same for their best friend. When Mapi asked if he had never wanted to get married, Luis glared at her like he used to and reached for one of the bottles of wine left over from the funeral. He hadn't stopped drinking since.

Having prepared dinner, she pushed the plate of fried food in front of Luis and shook his shoulder. 'Eat. It will sober you up.'

He grunted but stayed awake. His eyes rested on the plate of food. 'It smells good.'

'There is more if you want it.' Mapi sat down on a chair next to him and tucked into a plate of her own.

They ate in silence, and afterwards, she considered making him a strong cup of coffee, but decided against it as she wanted Luis to sleep through the night. She could no longer drink coffee late in the evenings; not even at home where she had a comfortable bed, never mind here, where she would be sleeping on an old lumpy sofa.

'I'll stay on the sofa,' Mapi said as she washed up the plates. 'We'll have to leave early as my daughter's train arrives in Málaga at eleven and we have to pick her up.' She dried her hands and put the towel away.

Luis was still sitting at the table. 'In a week I'll have nowhere to live,' he said, staring into space.

'What do you mean? This is your house.'

'Not anymore. I sold it at a stupid price a year ago, with the promise I could stay here for free until I died.' He pulled out a piece of paper from his pocket and handed it over. 'Now they want me out.'

She smoothed the crumbled piece of paper. *Unfortunate. They are doing the house up to sell. Three months' notice.* It was dated November 2002.

'Oh, Tío Luis. Why did you do that?' Mapi regretted the words as soon as they left her mouth. He would have asked himself the same during any sober moment he would have had.

'I had some debts to pay off and....' He took a deep breath. 'I didn't know what else to do. They made it sound like a good thing, and they seemed very honest. And I had probably had a drink.'

'There will be papers, though, for the sale, showing their part of the bargain.'

Luis looked up and shook his head. 'I can't find any mention of it in the papers.' He nodded towards a pile of papers to the side. 'Have a look if you like, but you won't find anything in there.'

'You go to bed now, and don't worry about it. I'll have a look through the papers. I'm sure it will all be fine.'

Luis stood up. 'It's not really for myself I feel sorry. I could sleep under a bridge—it's no more than I deserve—but Pepe left me the house so I would have somewhere to live until I died. That's what upsets me most.'

He threw a quick glance towards where the wine bottle Mapi had emptied earlier had stood before making his way upstairs to his bedroom. She hadn't checked for drink upstairs, but then again why would Luis hide bottles? It wasn't like there was normally anyone there to try and keep him sober.

Grabbing the papers, she went into the lounge where she'd made up the sofa earlier while the food cooked. Inside, Mapi was boiling that someone had taken advantage of her uncle. Even if there wasn't a legal leg to stand on, there must be a moral one. She'd make sure to find it, and if they didn't do what they had promised she'd make sure their actions were plastered on every paper from here to the North Pole.

Mapi put on her clown-patterned pyjamas, sat on top of the sheets and blanket that made up her bed, and started to read. She hadn't even reached the end of the first page before she fell asleep.

At some point in the night a chill had crept in, and cold and achy she crawled under the blanket. When her phone alarm went off it was early morning, still pitch dark. Once Mapi remembered where she was, she went into the kitchen and put the kettle on.

It was cool, and she wished she could go back to bed. The kitchen still smelled of bacon and garlic which would normally make her open all the windows and swear never to cook it again, now it just made her hungry. She found two mugs and measured out a loaded teaspoon of instant coffee into each one. It might not be the best coffee in the world, but it would be sure to wake them up. The grains dissolved in the steaming water and Mapi poured in a little milk before walking upstairs to wake up her uncle.

'Pásale,' Luis replied when she knocked on his door. *Good, at least he's up.* The room was dark, but from the light in the hallway she could make out her uncle sitting on the side of the bed. She flicked the light switch, but nothing happened.

Luis lifted his face from his hands, and said with a croak, 'It doesn't work.'

'Right.' Mapi made space on the cluttered bedside table and put the coffee mug down. 'Are you all right?'

'I have a headache.'

'I'm not surprised. I'll find you some tablets. Drink the coffee; it'll help wake you up.'

'I've been awake for a while,' he said, rummaging around in the gloom for the coffee cup. 'I had a dream and couldn't go back to sleep.'

Mapi opened the door to the hallway wide to let some light in, then went over to his wardrobe and found some clean, folded clothes. She wondered briefly who had laundered and put them away. Maybe her uncle stayed sober some days, or perhaps it was a neighbour. Perhaps a lady friend.

'We'll sort out the problem with this house, and then the dreams will probably go.'

Luis finished the coffee. 'These dreams are part of my life. Nothing will make them go away.'

Mapi turned around, curious. 'What are they about?'

Luis put the coffee cup down and slowly stood up before sitting back down. 'I'm sorry, Mapi. I don't think I can go. I feel a bit ... ill.'

'You're coming with me. You said you would, so you will. You can sleep in the car. Be ready, and showered, in twenty minutes.' Mapi went downstairs to make toast, leaving him sitting on the bed looking miserable.

When the sun rose over the Sierra Nevada Mountains, they were more than halfway to Málaga. Luis had dozed the whole way, and it wasn't until she left the main road for the N340, snaking its way along the coast, that he took an interest in the world they drove past.

'Do you know what happened on this road?' He spoke suddenly.

She looked around at the peaceful surroundings. 'No, I don't.'

Luis stayed silent as the sea shimmered in the early morning sun. Not getting a response, she glanced over. 'Go on; what happened here?'

'Never mind.' For a few minutes he fell silent once again. 'Your mamá hasn't told you?'

'Told me what?'

'That we were part of the exodus out of Málaga in 1937. That our mamá and brother died here. That this road was the start of everything.'

'Really? Tell me.'

'Doesn't matter now,' he said, closing his eyes to the world and his own memories.

Mapi needed him to be in a good mood for the party, so she didn't push it, no matter how much she wanted to, and drove on towards the Málaga train station. Once there they picked up her daughter, Mia, and drove towards the mountains and her mamá's eightieth birthday party.

~ 8 ~

**Alicante, Spain
February 1937 to May 1939**

It took seven days to walk to Alicante, and nobody was willing to give any one of them a lift. They were deeper into Republican territory now, so at least there were no major bombings. Still, they could hear plenty of planes in the sky and see warships out at sea, but they were either Republican or, if they were the enemy, they decided that in smaller numbers they weren't worth the ammunition.

Their feet were blistered and swollen and their stomachs ached with hunger and thirst, but the villages further north hadn't been overrun by thousands of refugees and so they didn't mind sharing their water or selling some of their food. Irena had some money tucked away, and from the way Señora Araya looked at her when she produced it Isabel could tell she wasn't happy. Irena had let her use her wedding ring to pay for their meal in Almería, when all along she'd had proper money hidden away.

By the time they got to Alicante they were tired and about to collapse, but they'd made it, and they were still alive. They set out immediately to locate the house of Señora Araya's cousin, Señora Alva, hoping she could take them in; her husband was away fighting somewhere up north. The house was tucked away from the hustle and bustle of the seafront and the main road, on a quiet cobbled road mostly made up of grey two-story houses that had once been white; inside, they were kept clean as ever. Located in the old town the shadow of the great Castillo de Santa Bárbara, full of legends and prisoners, perched high on a cliff above. Two cantinas and an old stone church which had been looted stood a little further down towards the sea; a panadería and carnicería could be found in the other direction. It was small and already full, yet when she'd heard what they'd been through she let them stay in the loft.

Alicante was busier than Málaga, different. Maybe it was that they had been in Málaga during the winter and were here in Alicante during the spring, but Isabel thought it lighter and somehow not as dirty. The training camp for the International Brigades that had come to help the Republic win the war was based in Albacete, not very far away from the town; different languages could be heard everywhere. Irena told Isabel how people from all over the world had come to help them win the war over fascism, and how they had helped save Madrid from being taken only a few months earlier.

The Señora started going to political meetings again, and Irena was out most of the time. This left Isabel and Luis in the house with Señora Alva, her mother-in-law Señora Fernandez, and her young son, Pepe. Luis, who had somehow buried the previous weeks' events deep down inside, ran around and played with Pepe, leaving a quiet Isabel to help around the house. She didn't mind as it took her mind off things, but Señora Alva's elderly mother-in-law snapped at her whenever she could. The old woman sat in the kitchen, sewing or peeling potatoes, and her beady little eyes followed Isabel around as she did her chores. There was nothing she could do about it, so Isabel ignored her as much as possible. She wouldn't be there for long because, any day now, papá would find them and they would go back home to La Quida.

'I know she's my cousin, but I haven't seen her for nearly ten years. Now she brings these children here and then goes out and about every day. How are we supposed to feed them?' Isabel heard Señora Alva talking to a neighbour just outside the front door and crept to the window in the hall above to better see and hear. 'We haven't got enough to feed our own.'

The neighbour was silent, then asked, 'That tall woman that's with her, is she a relative of yours too?'

'No. I don't know her at all. Irena's out most of the day and only returns late at night when everybody's asleep. I don't know what she does, and I don't want to ask.' Señora Alva leaned heavily on her broom.

'Well, I do,' the neighbour said, looking around to see if anybody was listening before she continued. 'I didn't want to say anything if she was related to you, but my husband saw her in a bar along the seafront, drinking and laughing with the foreign men—the International Brigade soldiers.'

'Paloma, I hope you're sure about what you're implying.' Señora Alva straightened herself up to her full height.

'As sure as I can be. I thought it would be better to tell you than let everybody gossip behind your back.'

Señora Alva nodded, as if it was what she'd expected all along. 'I'll tell my cousin that her friend has to leave. We can't have someone like that in the house.' She sighed. 'It's a shame though; that woman is the only one who brings food into the house.'

'Yes, Elisa, and from where does she get it? You wouldn't like her to be in any town near your husband, would you?'

For a long moment Señora Alva stared down at her newly swept step before sighing again. 'Maybe she just has a drink with them. These days, everything is different: women vote, drink, and fight.' She paused before dropping to a whisper. 'I'll have a word with her about it, but if she's not taking money from them it might be all right.'

Paloma appeared to think it over for a moment and, sensing her neighbour's reluctance to get rid of her lodger, she agreed with her. 'It's not good, but I suppose it's bearable if no money changes hands.'

Señora Alva nodded, smiling at the thought of keeping her small but valuable supply of extra food. Isabel, still sitting by the window above the front door, was relieved, glad that Irena was staying; she was almost never there anyway. They were in the midst of fighting a war and staying alive must be the first and most important thing. She didn't like Señora Alva much. She had a hard and wrinkled hard face, but Isabel didn't think she could be that old as her son was the same age as Luis. Her wrinkles and sour mouth probably came from never smiling, and Isabel hoped they wouldn't have to stay too long.

Apart from perhaps an hour in the afternoon, the sun did not reach their road at all, so Isabel sometimes sneaked out on her own to get a little sunlight. She'd found a large stone she could climb up and look out over the sea, watching the motor vehicles and the soldiers that moved along the main road while feeling the sun on her face. She liked to sit on the warm stone and dream that her papá would spot her and come running up—how surprised and happy she would be; how he would make everything all right. He would smile as he carried her back to the house, where they'd collect Luis and say thank you to Señoras Araya and Alva before they went back home.

'Isabel, come over here.' She opened her eyes and saw Luis and Pepe over by the abandoned broken fishing boat, which had somehow ended upside down on the other side of the street. Reluctantly, she slid down from the stone and walked over.

'Look what's inside,' Luis said, nudging her towards the small triangular space that was the only way to get inside the boat.

'I'm not going in,' she said, turning her nose up at the smell that came out from under the craft.

The two boys looked at each other. 'It's a dead person.'

'How do you know? Did you go under there?'

'We always do. It's our secret hideaway, and he wasn't there two days ago. The sun must have cooked him and that's why it smells so bad.'

Isabel walked further away and took a deep breath of fresh air. 'Go and tell those policemen over there.' She pointed across the street. 'They'll have to investigate.'

'But they'll find our place.'

'Would you rather spend time in there with a dead body?'

The boys sighed and went to fetch the policemen, who came over and glanced inside while holding their breath.

'Yes, there's a body in there all right.' He looked at the three children standing as close as they could to the boat. 'Now, you go and stand over there.'

His partner pointed away from the boat. 'But don't leave without talking to me first. Understand?'

'Who is it?' Pepe asked.

'I don't know. We'll have a look. Now go over there so you're not in our way.'

All three nodded and backed reluctantly away while the two policemen got assistance from some militia in turning the boat over. With a bang it rolled onto its side.

The activity had drawn a bit of a crowd, but when they saw the partly decayed body exposed to the sunlight everyone took a step back. His head had been nearly severed from his body, and he wore dark trousers and what had once been a white cotton shirt.

Very quickly chatter started up as to who it could be, and even though the smell was awful, people edged closer to have a good look. After a while the onlookers dispersed—a dead body nobody recognised wasn't big news—and a van arrived to take the victim away.

Isabel and the boys watched as the coroners left, and then the policeman asked where they lived before sending them on their way back home.

'Well, where are we going to have our headquarters now?' Pepe asked Luis. 'That was the best place.'

'We'll find somewhere just as good.' He turned to Isabel. 'Who do you think it was?'

'I don't know. Maybe someone important who got killed by fascists hiding in the city,' she said, joking.

'Do you really think so?'

'No. It's probably someone who got killed for food or money. Or maybe he'd blackmailed somebody and the person he was blackmailing decided to kill him.'

'You're being stupid now.'

'It might be true,' said Pepe.

Isabel left them at the end of their street, still discussing the origins of the dead man, while she walked slowly back to the house. She knew she'd be told off for staying away so long, but reflected how it was funny they only had one set of clothes to wear yet there was always washing to do—and it was always her job to do it. She didn't mind so much now, as it helped pass the time until the war was over and they could go back home.

The following day two policemen came to the house, asking about the discovery of the body. The victim turned out to be the editor of the local communist paper. Nobody had any idea who had done it or why, but with the internal war going on between the CNT/FAI militia and the communists it might as well be an anarchist as a fascist fifth columnist.

When they realised that neither Isabel nor the boys had any further information to give the policemen left. Luis and Pepe ran after them, asking questions until they disappeared around a corner.

Isabel then went with Señora Alva to the hospital, where they washed bandages and cleaned wards for the war effort. They didn't speak much, but Señora Alva kept gossiping with others; there wasn't much going on in the neighbourhood she didn't know about. At least once a day she discussed the man who lived on the corner of their road. He seemed to spend most of his day sitting by the window looking out over the steps leading up to the Castillo. The Castillo held quite a few prisoners, and his house was perfectly positioned for finding out who went in and who came out. Señora Alva was convinced he was a spy for Franco. She'd even informed the authorities, but they had told her he'd been injured and was trustworthy. Quite an unusual stance for the authorities to take, she said, as it didn't normally require very much for someone to be taken in on a charge of spying. However, Señora Alva didn't give up, and every time she walked past, she caught his eye and glared as hard as she could.

One good thing about helping at the hospital was that they got a proper meal in return. Not that it really counted, as when they returned home Isabel was excluded from the evening meal, which she still had to help serve. To be fair, Señora Alva didn't eat in the evenings either, but the rest of the family did, and Isabel's stomach growled every time.

They had been in Alicante just over a year when everything changed. Even though bombs still fell and there was a lack of food, it had seemed to Isabel as if everything had calmed down a little.

One night, as they were going to sleep, she turned to Señora Araya and asked. 'I'm fifteen now. Would you say that is grown-up?' There were seven of them who used the room, so she whispered as to not disturb the others.

'Very grown-up. Are you planning to marry or join the army?'

'Nothing like that.' Isabel smiled a little in the dark. 'But I would like to go home again. I promised I'd find papá, and everything seems calmer now.'

'It's not calmer. We are losing battle after battle and the fascists are still murdering almost everybody in the towns they take. Just because we've been lucky for the time being doesn't mean it's all over, Isabel. I promise you your papá won't be there.'

'I just thought that perhaps we could walk through the forests and over the mountains to get home. We don't have to use the roads. And if our old house isn't there anymore, we can build a new one. You and Irena can come, too. You'd like it there.'

'That's enough now. Go to sleep and tomorrow you can come with me to the committee building and help out.'

Disappointed her plan had been pushed to the side so quickly, Isabel closed her eyes and eventually fell asleep.

Still slightly stung the following morning, Isabel accompanied Señora Araya to the committee building in the city centre. It was an old thin building that had survived the bombing raids, fully intact. Once there, the Señora had to go out and so Isabel moved the chair on which she'd been asked to wait closer to the open window. The room smelled of cigarette smoke, and one of the walls was lined with cabinets in which people kept on coming in to find or return folders. She wasn't sure why she was just waiting for the Señora and felt there must be something she could do help, but she didn't want to ask, and so simply waited by the window for Señora Araya to return.

She looked down at the dress she wore, which was blue and didn't have any holes; it was clean, too. Irena had brought it back for her, although she didn't know where it had come from. In one pocket there had been a small purse containing twenty pesetas. She'd tried to give them back to Irena, thinking she must know where to return it, but she'd just bent down and whispered it was her money and she should keep it for a rainy day. She said every girl should have something put aside so they didn't have to support themselves doing things they didn't want to do. Isabel wasn't quite sure what she'd meant, but she'd nodded as if she did and thanked Irena. She'd hidden the money in the wall and not told anybody else.

Tired of sitting by the window and doing nothing, Isabel got up and asked the lady at the desk where she could find the Señora. She was told she'd gone to the market but should be back shortly. A bored Isabel thanked the lady and went back to the chair by the window.

Only a few minutes later the now-familiar sound of planes reached her through the open window, followed by the whining of falling bombs. From the doorway, a spindly middle-aged man shouted at her to get to the shelter.

Isabel followed the others towards the stairs to the basement. In front of her was the receptionist, carrying a stack of folders. She gratefully accepted Isabel's offer of help. The three interconnecting areas of the basement were small, and they all had to squeeze into the dark and damp-smelling rooms.

She ended up on the far side of the basement, and in the light from a lantern someone lit, Isabel saw the strained faces crammed in all around her. She was too far away from the doorway, and an escape route, to feel comfortable. Her foot began tapping the floor and she felt nauseous. The bombs fell and the building shook with each one, filling the air with dust from cement and plaster. She coughed and tried to catch her breath, but with her back against the wall she slumped down to the floor.

'Put this over your mouth and nose,' said the lady with the files, handing her a scarf. Isabel did as she was told and concentrated on her breathing. In and out, in and out....

A nervous silence lay over the thirty or so people crammed into the basement shelter. Some looked around the walls, as if to make sure they were still standing, while others stared in front of them, hoping they would once again be lucky enough to carry on living. At some point, someone started singing while others started discussing the lack of air raid shelters and anti-aircraft guns, or the lack of progress in their original programme of revolutionary aims and goals.

By the time the raid stopped, loud discussions had taken off and continued as everyone filtered out of the basement. The room had almost cleared by the time Isabel felt able to stand up. She shook her head to try and clear her head of the ringing noise, but it wouldn't go away. Covered in dust she joined the others outside the building, where they had all stopped to stare. The far end of the road was devastated. All around them plumes of smoke and dust rose over the collapsed buildings. They had been the lucky ones. Sirens echoed through the streets as people emerged from whatever shelters they'd found and ran towards the injured and the dead.

Isabel didn't know whether to run back to the house to see if everyone was all right, or to the market where Señora Araya had gone. In the end, she followed the other women from the committee building as they moved down the street, spreading out as they walked.

The market square was only a few blocks away and had taken the brunt of the bombing. There were fires everywhere, and both men and women wailed into the foul air as they found their loved ones. Isabel followed the remaining two women from the office as they tried to help the injured lying around the square. When the air finally started to clear she went looking for Señora Araya.

When Isabel found her, she wished she hadn't. Her body was being carried to a corner of the square where it could be identified. Isabel fell to her knees next to the Señora as they carefully put her down on the ground. Apart from a cut on her forehead she looked peacefully asleep. Isabel used her scarf to clean the dust from her face, touching her cheek. Since Málaga she'd become so fond of Señora Araya, this woman who had taken care of her and Luis when most would have handed the responsibility over to someone else. She sat holding her hand when one of the men who had carried her over asked, 'Did you know her, Señorita?

'She's my aunt.' She looked up at him. 'She's taken care of us.'

Sympathetic, the man put his hand on her shoulder. 'I'm so sorry. I really am.'

Apart from Irena, the house was empty. Pepe had been badly injured and they had all gone to the hospital. Irena didn't know what was wrong, but Luis had gone with him, refusing to leave his side.

'The Señora is dead,' Isabel told Irena without ceremony. They sat at the table in silence for a while as Irena took it in.

'They are picking us off one by one,' she said, lighting a cigarette. 'And our government is letting them.'

'But the fascists have all the new weapons. How can we fight them without ... without anything to fight with?' Isabel echoed the words of one of the men in the basement.

'I don't know.' Irena sighed and looked out the dusty window. 'We can't stay here now Señora Araya is gone.'

That was something Isabel hadn't even thought about. 'They wouldn't put us on the street?'

'Times are hard for them too, and maybe they'd let Luis stay but you'd be a burden.'

'Where would we go?' She still remembered the conversation she'd had with the Señora about returning to La Quida, so she didn't mention that option. She didn't want to leave the house they'd lived in for more than a year, but she also didn't want to be a burden to anyone else. The last few weeks, ever since she'd received the dress from Irena, she'd felt they had a connection even though they hadn't always got on. She was a link to the past, and she needed to hold on to that now there were so few left.

'I know somewhere we can stay,' Irena said, standing. 'Wait for Luis and I'll come fetch you in the morning.' With that she left, and a few minutes later Isabel started clearing the building of dust and broken glass from the windows.

***

The large loft she now shared with Irena was bomb-damaged and always gloomy. Seagulls nested on the roof, their feet clicking and scraping the tiles at all hours. The noise drove them mad, and they regularly picked up the broom and hit the ceiling with the handle to shoo them away. The gulls took no notice.

Bare electrical wires hung from the ceiling, disappearing underneath the rough floorboards that frequently gave them splinters. Isabel thought the wires could have been cut down as the building hadn't had electricity since the beginning of the war, and it was highly unlikely to be restored until it was over. Neither she nor Irena wanted to do the cutting, so they left them where they were. The room's one saving grace was a small, low window that looked out over the road to the sea.

Early every morning Isabel would plat her long hair and carefully navigate her way down the broken stairs, stepping in just the right places to avoid breaking through the rotten steps. Then she'd hurry along to the CNT committee building, where she helped with paperwork and ran errands throughout the day. In return she got a meal and felt as though she was finally part of something bigger. It was all very unofficial, however, as she was not yet old enough to join, but it helped to know it was the same organisation papá belonged to. Often, members of the CNT/FAI militia would come by and she would ask if they knew a José Mosca. Nobody ever did.

Whenever there was a bombing raid Isabel made sure she entered the basement last so she could stand right by the door. She never got used to the raids and every time they filtered out from the basement, having once again survived, she swore she would never go in there again.

In the evenings she went to Señora Alva's house to visit Luis, who had wanted to stay with Pepe. Isabel hadn't been too happy leaving him, but Señora Alva had persuaded her it was better for him to stay in a safe and secure house. Isabel had wanted to argue it had recently been bomb-damaged, and therefore not all that safe, but she hadn't because she wanted her brother to be as happy as he could be. It had been made clear, however, in the nicest of ways, that it would be best all round if she left with Irena.

The room where they lived was large enough for both her and Irena to have some private space at each end. Irena's was at the far end because it was partly screened by a brick wall, while Isabel was closest to the little window. Some nights Irena brought men back home, and Isabel had to pull a blanket over her head and try her best to quickly fall asleep. But she couldn't complain too much, as that was how Irena paid their rent and didn't ask her for a peseta.

Isabel never mentioned Irena at work, because what she did for money was seen as the lowest a woman could fall. The fascists viewed all Republican women as whores, and people like Irena just proved them right. Her work kept her busy and most nights she came home so tired she could have slept through anything, not even waking when Irena returned. She wondered what those men thought when Irena asked them to be quiet so they wouldn't wake up her friend, daughter, or sister. Her role in Irena's life varied on her mood and amount of drinks she'd had.

The war was going badly, but there was still hope because, well, there had to be. The city was bombed regularly, and they became, together with the rest of the citizens, very good at hearing the planes approach. This only gave a tiny amount of extra time, but with no air raid warnings and no anti-aircraft guns to protect them, they needed every second they could get; especially living on the top floor, as they did.

Autumn arrived and still no good news came their way.

'I'm going to miss them you know,' Irena said one day as they sat at a bar. The mellow October sunshine was still warm, and the bar's radio was blaring news and music.

'Who?'

'The International Brigades. They're being sent home. Such brave men,' Irena said. 'Such good payers.' She burst out laughing. 'I'm sorry, Bella, I'm sure you will have a good life, but for some of us it's too late. We have to make the best of what we have to survive.'

'You don't have to do it; you could come work with the committee or up at the hospital. They give you a meal each day.'

Irena smiled her crooked smile. 'It's not for me, Bella.'

Isabel didn't like to be called Bella but knew there was no point saying so. 'So, are you going to do this forever?'

'Forever? Who plans for that in this world? Maybe once I did, because once, I know it's hard to believe, I was like you are now: a loved daughter. Then things started going wrong. My mamá died, my papá started drinking, and I married a bad man who left me while I was pregnant with Rosa. There were no jobs, and I couldn't let her starve. If I had to, I would do the same again. Well, I'd make sure I wasn't in Málaga when the doors of hell opened, but apart from that....' She lit a cigarette and offered one to Isabel.

It was the first time Isabel had been treated as a proper grown-up, so she accepted. Not knowing how to smoke she blew air into it and Irena couldn't stop laughing.

'You suck on it. Drag the smoke into your lungs. You'll cough at first, but it gets easier.'

She did as Irena said and nearly coughed up her lungs.

Some soldiers walking past laughed at her. 'Filthy habit for a girl,' one of them said.

'Thank you for your comments. They have been duly noted,' Irena threw back sarcastically. 'Seriously,' she continued. 'I don't know what's going to happen now that such a large part of our army is leaving.'

'They wouldn't let them go if they thought we'd lose.'

'They don't want to go; they're being made to. No doubt for some ridiculous political reason.'

When Isabel tried the cigarette again it went better. How grown-up she felt, sitting with a cigarette in one hand and a coffee substitute in the other. By the time Irena paid the bill and they started walking back to their room, she was quite good at it. It didn't taste nice, but that didn't matter as cigarettes were hard to come by and she didn't have any more. Still, she now knew how to do it.

As autumn turned to winter and winter to spring, Barcelona, followed by Madrid, fell to the Nationalists. The Republicans knew they would lose the war. The city was overrun with thousands and thousands of ragged and tired soldiers and officials, writers and intellectuals, from all over the country and all hoping for an escape from what they knew would be their worst nightmare. The only trouble was that there was nowhere left to run. The port at Alicante was the end of the road, the last free area in Spain. All of them were waiting for ships to come and rescue them.

Isabel and Irena sat by the little window, looking out over the harbour that was so full of people some fell into the water.

'Madrid has gone and they're almost here,' Isabel said. She'd been working for days trying to help the refugees. Fresh in her memory was their entry into Almería only two years before, and the desperation they had then felt. She'd hoped to be able to convince Irena to let some stay in their room, but she'd given a flat 'no.' As it was really her room, Isabel didn't feel as though she could argue.

'We have nowhere to run. It's an understatement to say I'm scared, Isabel.'

As they sat at the window, another influx of sorry-looking Republican soldiers who had never stood a chance of winning against the German and Italian troops and weapons, arrived. If Franco hadn't received help, everything would all have been all right; this awful, horrid mess would never have happened.

Irena sank down on the floor and leaned her head back against the low frame. 'What are we going to do?'

'When they've won, they won't kill people anymore. Why would they? They would have taken over the government and got what they wanted. It will just go back to the way it was before. I'm really looking forward to going back home.'

'Isabel, they won't let us forget this. They will get their revenge on us all.'

'But they started the war; how can they blame the Republic? That's stupid.'

'Maybe, but they will. We should be prepared for the absolute worst. Don't you remember the road from Málaga, and how they killed everybody? Women, children, old men?'

Isabel didn't want to think about that, about how all facts pointed to Irena's version of what the future held.

'We haven't got much food or water. Is there anywhere we can get some just in case we need it?' Isabel didn't worry about Luis and his welfare as he was only a small boy of ten and Señora Alva was clever enough to look after her family.

'There's enough here for a week or so. I've been stockpiling over the last few months. And we have cigarettes.' Irena threw a packet in the air. 'It won't do our cash-flow any good, being stuck here. When they arrive they're sure to rifle through every house and steal everything in it.'

They'd hidden their valuables in a hole in the wall, putting a piece of wood in front. That's where she kept the photo of papá, and the money Irena had given her with the new dress. Irena had hidden her things somewhere else. Both hoped nobody would find their valuables.

For the rest of the day they felt like the observers of a lost world as they sat watching the people in the port.

It rained most of the night. On the beach below the poor, trapped refugees lit fires on the beach to keep warm, still hoping against all odds the promised boats would come. Only two ships had got through Franco's blockade and, as one took on so many passengers it looked as though it might sink, the other one took only a handful before sailing off. They were both British vessels.

The following day, March 31, 1939, the fascists walked into the city and made their presence known. Isabel felt like she was watching a film. The war was over, and they'd lost. The fascist Italian soldiers hoisted the new flag under Franco's regime and cordoned off the port, waiting for the thousands of people to give up.

With glazed eyes, Isabel and Irena watched as some Republican men and women committed suicide rather than be taken prisoner, shooting, stabbing, or drowning themselves in desperation. A fascist battleship approached the port and ordered the Republicans to leave, but nobody moved until the ship fired its machine gun over their heads. Finally, they gave up, and the two thousand remaining Republicans who had fought for their freedom were either executed then and there or dragged away to various camps.

Then the fascists' purge of the city really began.

They had soon taken over public buildings and started making lists of people to execute or arrest. Over the next few days they arrested thousands, dragging people from their homes for the smallest of reasons: if they'd voted for the Popular Front in 1936, if they'd ever belonged to a union, if they'd been on strike at any time since 1934. If in anyway one had been involved in the Republican effort to stop Franco and his army, you were fair game. The new laws said so.

It was only a matter of time until somebody would come bursting into the loft where they lived. But when they did, it still took Irena and Isabel by surprise. They'd stayed indoors since the fascists had entered the city, and most of that time Isabel had sat on the floor by the window, a big knot in her stomach, knowing Irena felt the same way. Shots were heard throughout the night, and there was no way of knowing who fired them.

Isabel and Irena sat quietly, staring at each other while waiting to see what would happen. The soldiers started with the rooms downstairs, occupied by a family of four women and a whole batch of children, before moving upwards.

Irena instructed Isabel. 'Just keep calm. Whatever they do, remember to keep calm.' They stood up very quietly, hands showing so that they wouldn't think they had any weapons.

The sound of wood breaking came from the floor below, followed by swearing. 'You, up there, come down.'

They looked at each other and Isabel smiled. 'They can't get up the stairs.'

'They will eventually. We'll have to go down.'

A hail of bullets came crashing through the floor and they both screamed.

'We're coming! There's no need to shoot,' Irena shouted.

With clammy hands raised above their heads they walked out onto the rickety landing. Below them were three men in uniform, two with guns in their hands.

Slowly, Isabel and Irena went down the stairs one at the time, avoiding the ones they knew would break.

'Have you got identity papers,' asked the tall one who seemed to be in charge.

They both shook their heads as he took out a notebook and a pen.

'You need to tell me your names and where you're from. Then you need to tell me if you've been involved in the war against Spain, or committed any other crimes since 1934, such as belonging to a union. Let me warn you that if you don't tell the truth we will take you outside and shoot you right now. Do you understand?'

They both nodded.

'Right, we'll start with you.' He looked at Isabel.

Her mind had gone blank and she couldn't remember what he wanted to know.

'Your name.'

'Isabel Mosca. I'm sixteen years old and from a village called Quidera. I don't belong to a union.'

'Where are your parents?'

'My mamá is dead and I don't know where my papá is.'

'Were they fighting against Spain?'

Isabel's voice shook as she tried to keep herself from crying. 'My papá was a soldier.'

'What's his name?'

'José Mosca, Señor.'

He looked at her for a moment before turning his attention to Irena.

'My name is Irena Santos. I'm from Málaga, and I am a member of the communist party.'

Isabel saw the look in her eyes as she admitted her political membership; she must have known what would happen because her gaze had turned to steel.

When the soldiers led her away Isabel stayed frozen where she stood. She and Irena had become close over the last ten months, and even though they were so different they had understood each other better than anyone else.

She doubted Irena would be back soon.

They're picking us off, one by one.

***

Isabel stayed in their room until she couldn't bear to any longer. She had to see Luis, and that thought finally pushed her out of the loft. If she was braver she would try to find out where Irena had been taken straight away, but she didn't feel brave. She was sixteen years old, the age Pilar had been when she got married and joined the militia; she was a grown-up, but didn't feel like one. Even after everything that had happened since she left her home in the mountains, she'd never felt as alone as she did then.

All the doors of the other rooms in the house were closed, and she heard only silence on the other side. Taking a deep breath, Isabel opened the front door. On the street were motor cars and tanks; everywhere there were Italian and Spanish Nationalist soldiers

Grey clouds sped across the mid-April sky, but the wind held a spring warmth. Along the seafront were soldiers with rifles at the ready, standing guard. Across the road, by the untended flowerbeds, a couple of young boys were running around chasing each other. Their clothes were torn and dirty, but they were laughing. For a few moments Isabel watched, savouring the sound of playful laughter, which she hadn't heard for a long time. Then she walked along the road, turning into Calle Villavieja.

There were some civilians on this street, but all kept their heads down and moved quickly along to wherever it was they were going. Gunfire could be heard from a few streets away and she increased her speed, zigzagging through the narrow streets until she reached Señora Alva's house.

For a moment she didn't think she would be let in, but finally Señora Alva opened the door.

'Quickly,' she said, ushering Isabel inside and shutting the door. 'Have you got any food?'

'No. There are some cigarettes, but no food.'

They sat in the lounge next to Pepe's bed, which had been there since he lost his leg in the bombing. She was so relieved to see Luis playing some game with his friend, but to her surprise, apart from a hello when she came in, he didn't pay her any attention. It had been almost two weeks since she'd seen him last, and she didn't know whether to be happy or sad at his cool welcome.

'You shouldn't have come. Stay away from the streets if you can.'

'But I couldn't. I had to see you were all right.'

Both women stayed quiet for a few minutes, watching the two boys play.

'They arrested Irena and took her away.'

'Well, that's hardly surprising. The life she lived ... I hope she didn't have a bad influence on you.'

'It wasn't that; she was a member of the communist party. I didn't know.'

Señora Alva nodded. 'They were here asking, too. They very kindly informed me that as my husband isn't here I may be fined or arrested in his place. I fear there are many dark days ahead, my girl.'

Isabel looked up to where a crucifix hung proudly on the wall, as though it had never been taken down and spat upon—which she knew many of the Republicans, including her parents, had done.

'Better safe than sorry, I say,' Señora Alva said, noticing Isabel's glance. 'If they want to believe we believe, that's fine. It doesn't mean we actually have to. Once they have had their fill of victory it can come back down. I'm just glad it somehow didn't get thrown away back in '36.'

Isabel changed topics, whispering to Señora Alva. 'Why is Luis ignoring me?'

'He's angry you haven't been to see him for over ten days. I've tried to explain to him what happened, but I think he was scared you'd left him.'

'I don't know what to do, Señora.' Once she said those words she couldn't stop herself: all her worries and fears, that had for so long been locked up inside, came flooding out. 'I live in constant fear they'll come arrest me for some minor offence, because they don't seem to need much of a reason. There's no money, no food, and now that Irena's not around to pay the rent I'm likely to get thrown out of the room, too. I thought when the war ended, no matter how hard it was that we lost, it would be okay because we could go back home. There we'd be all right. In our village where papá could find us. I just don't think I have the strength to see it through. To last until we can leave.'

Señora Alva's stern eyes hadn't left her face. 'You're a young girl; if you think about giving up, what hope is there for the rest of us? Think about the poor soldiers held in prisoner-of-war camps that, if the rumours are to be believed, are worse than death; think about all those poor refugees they took from the beach last week, and what they must be going through.' Her voice softened a little. 'I know you two have had it hard, but so has everybody else. We survive—that's what we do—and we live to fight another day.' She turned her gaze to Luis. 'Your sister is staying with us for a few days, until she finds somewhere else to live.'

Luis's eyes lit up. 'Really?'

Isabel nodded, giving a hint of a smile. 'It would seem so.'

He turned back to Pepe. 'She tells really good stories, you'll see.'

'I have to pick some things up, but I'll come back straight away ... If that's all right?'

'Be careful out there. Remember most people will tell the authorities anything if it will save their own skins, including lying about friends and neighbours.'

'Irena wouldn't do such a thing. I know she wouldn't.'

'It's not just her I mean. Don't trust anybody.'

Isabel reluctantly left the house and walked back to the seafront. She had to hurry if she was to get back to Luis before darkness and the early curfew set in.

When she reached the loft, she noticed another one of the steps had broken. It hadn't been her; both she and Irena had them down to a fine art. 'Hello, is anybody up there?'

There was no answer, no sound. She walked carefully up the steps, and with her heart in her mouth pushed open the door. The room was empty. Everything was gone: their mattresses, the cigarette packets Irena had managed to get hold of, even their two mugs and the metal lids they'd used as plates.

Isabel's gaze flew over to the wall where they'd kept their valuables. The piece of wood they'd wedged in front was lying on the floor. She put her hand into the hole, feeling around the cavity. It too was empty.

She'd only been gone a couple of hours. Somebody must have heard her leave and decided to take their chance now that Irena was also gone. How did they know where to look? How would she explain this to Irena if she ever came out of prison? Isabel sank to the floor and stared into space. Gone was all she had in the world: the money she'd got from Irena, and the photo of papá. Now she had nothing but the grubby old dress she wore. She knew Irena had hidden some money, but she also knew it wasn't in their room and she hadn't told Isabel where she'd left it.

Come on, pull yourself together. If you stay here you'll starve to death, and your body will rot on the floorboards. Nobody would care, would they? *Luis would.* That is, if he ever found out. He might just wait forever for her to come back.

After a minute Isabel stood back up. Señora Alva was right not to trust anyone, and she wouldn't from now on. Doing a final search, she found on the floor behind the door, the photo of her papá, thrown to one side as something of no value. Still, she was pleased that whoever had robbed them had decided they didn't want it. She put it in her pocket and, with a last look around, walked back down the stairs.

The door to the apartment of the family downstairs clicked shut, as if they'd been spying. They would know Irena had been taken away, and nobody had wanted to upset her. So, the loud-mouthed mamá behind the door had taken her chance, and succeeded.

Isabel spat at the door, shouting, 'I know it was you. Shame on you all for turning into thieves.' But she left it at that, as there wasn't anything else she could do. She hoped they got no pleasure from anything they took. Filled with anger she slammed the tall front door behind her as hard as she could.

She hadn't even reached the end of the road before she was stopped by a gang of bored soldiers standing on the corner. One of them had stepped right in front of her, nearly causing her to walk into him. She was almost as tall as him, and she noticed half his ear was missing.

'Where are you going, Rojo?'

'I'm going home, Señor.' She knew it wouldn't do to argue.

'Do you know there's a curfew, and that you're breaking it? Do you know the penalty for that?'

'I'm sorry. I didn't know it had yet started. I'll go straight home.'

'That's not good enough. The only people out after dark are enemies of Spain.' He grabbed hold of her hair and pushed Isabel to her knees. The trembling fear she felt inside was only held in place by Irena's advice to keep calm, no matter what happened. 'I think we'll take you to the station.'

Still gripping her hair, he pulled her back up and started walking towards the alleyway. Bent over, Isabel stumbled along behind him, trying her best not to shout in pain as he pulled her along the nearly empty street. His friends suddenly stopped laughing and started shouting.

'Hey, there they are.' One pointed towards two men in civilian clothes, who were being chased by another fascist soldier. The two men were headed towards the beach, and Isabel was thrown to the side as the man holding her hair let go. His friends had got a head start, running towards the unfortunate men on the beach.

The soldier should a warning at Isabel as he ran to join his friends in the chase. 'Next time!'

It took only a second for her to get back on her feet and sprint down the alleyway.

When Isabel was far enough away, she stopped and slumped against a wall. Tears poured down her cheeks as she fell onto the cobbled street. Her body shook, and she felt cold and sick. There was a buzzing in her ears and she struggled not to faint. She sat there for several minutes, concentrating on her breathing, knowing she had to move before some other soldier came along. If the curfew really had started, as the men had said, she would be in trouble. She struggled back onto her feet and stumbled along the darkening alleyways until she reached Señora Alva's house. When Señora Alva asked what was the matter, she lied and said she was upset about the robbery. She was upset about it, but it was the soldiers that had scared her. The house felt safe though, knowing there were people there with her calmed her down. Receiving a piece of bread and beans for her dinner was comforting.

That night she slept better than she had in ages. Even after everything that had happened, Isabel felt herself relax while she lay on the sofa, her brother's feet in her face. The rhythmic breathing of the two boys sent her into a deep and dreamless sleep, and she didn't wake until the Señora came in to announce they were all going to church.

Isabel hadn't told them about her lucky escape the previous night. There was no doubt in her mind what would have happened if those two men hadn't run past and, by their own beliefs and convictions, saved her. She couldn't remember if she had heard any shots ring out; she couldn't even remember running away. The only person she could talk to about anything was in prison, and she felt too much shame to even admit what could have happened to Señora Alva. Anyway, nothing had happened, so there was nothing to talk about.

She followed as Señora Alva led her household, apart from Pepe, down the street to the church on the corner. It had been badly damaged, and the beautiful relics inside had been looted at the beginning of the war. Isabel knew the priest had run away soon after the fascist uprising in Alicante had failed and he'd realised just how dangerous his position was. He had now returned, and his face was screwed up with distaste and hate as the very people he'd been forced to run from returned, meek as sheep, to his church wanting God's forgiveness. He must know that most didn't want to go, and only did so out of fear. Señora Alva had told them to keep their head down and to be careful when they confessed their sins. Villagers knew the priest had spent the previous few days pointing out those he deemed anti-Catholic to the authorities, thereby condemning them to death. So Señora Alva brought along everyone she could.

None of the children, including Isabel, knew any hymns, psalms, or church etiquette, so Señora Alva had given them a quick lesson before leaving the house.

The church doors, which had been broken and left swinging in the wind ever since Isabel had arrived in Alicante, were now repaired and the interior had been tidied up. There remained only two rows of pews to sit on, but they had been reserved for the winners, for the fascists. The rest had to kneel for the whole mass. To make it more painful, to allow them to suffer a little more, gravel had been strewn over the area so that small stones dug into their knees. When the whole sorry mass was over, after the priest had preached about God's wrath, about the glory of the Catholic church, and about the joys of Franco's victory, they had been on their knees for over three hours. Pain seared through every Republican there, all apart from the holier-than-thou priest and the four who sat on the pews. Slowly, they rose and joined the queue for the exit, where the priest greeted them.

'Señora Alva. I expect we'll see you and your family for confession?'

'Of course, Father.' She bowed her head slightly as she spoke.

'We will have to work around the clock to listen to all the sins that have been committed the last few years. Don't you agree?'

'I do, Father. Indeed I do.'

They moved along the line until they were outside the church. At the bottom of the stone steps stood the man from the window; the man Señora Alva had been convinced was a spy. The one she'd tried to get arrested.

If Señora Alva noticed him she didn't show it.

'So, you've given in to them?' Paloma, the woman from next door whispered as they walked past. 'Your husband, if he's still alive, would be ashamed of you.'

'Don't you tell me what my husband is or isn't. He wouldn't want us all dragged off to prison either, would he?' Señora Alva ushered everybody into the house, pausing on the step. 'We do what has to be done, Paloma. We don't have to like it.'

Her neighbour nodded as Señora Alva looked down the street to where the man still stood, a smirk on his face.

'You shouldn't have annoyed him. No Republican would smile like that now,' Paloma said.

'Well, what's done is done. I may have to bow to the priest and the fascists, but I won't bow to him.'

'You know, they have set up a place for denunciations.'

'Have they? I wouldn't expect anything else from these people.'

'Take care, Elisa.' Paloma squeezed her arm. 'Don't let that temper of yours get you into trouble.'

'Me? You're the one who insulted me for going to church,' Señora Alva said.

Paloma laughed and went back inside, shutting the door behind her.

~ 9 ~

**Andalucía, Spain
February 2003**

'I don't want to go for a walk, Mapi. I've had a nagging headache all morning. We have enough food for today.' Isabel remained in her old, patched-up armchair. 'We'll go out tomorrow.'

Mapi knew how stubborn her mamá could be, so decided to tell her about the party. She didn't mention Luis.

'And they're all up at the house now?' Isabel feigned surprise.

'Yes.'

'And Mia, too?'

'I picked her up from Málaga this morning.'

Isabel sighed and stood up. 'Well, then I have no choice but to go.'

Mapi smiled. She could see her mamá was excited so many people had made the effort just for her.

'But I need to put something else on. Would you really have let me go in this old house frock?'

Isabel's legs and stamina were not what they once had been, and she struggled to get up the hill towards La Quida. They stopped on the way to look in at the house that had been their home for most of Mapi's life; it was being turned into a holiday home by some people from England.

'It's not the same now,' Isabel said as they stood by the gate. The garden was overgrown, and bags of sand and tools had been left by a workbench, making it look as though the new owners were reluctant to make it over. *Our home....*

'Nothing stays the same forever,' Mapi replied. 'It will always be a place of fond memories; for you, me, and papá.'

Her mamá squeezed her hand and they stood in silence looking at the house for a few more moments. 'There is something you should know, Mapi. I've been a coward for so many years and still, now, I can't....'

'Mamá, what is it? You can tell me anything.'

'I know, but some things are hard to say.... I've written it down just in case I'm too much of a coward to tell you. We'll talk about it later.' Isabel turned to her daughter and smiled. 'Right now we have a party to go to.'

Music and laughter were the first things they heard as they emerged from the wooded path and La Quida came into view. Lights were strung across the old garden, and what seemed like the whole village was there, talking and laughing together.

Isabel stopped and smiled. The garden had been cleared, and tables and chairs set out on the grass. Even the sun had put in a performance, bathing La Quida in its golden light. It had been too long since she'd been here. As they walked down the path, the party noticed their arrival and started singing 'Cumpleaños Feliz.' She saw her granddaughter, Mia, and smiled wider. So many people; people she loved, people she didn't know. They were here for her, gathered at her old home.

After a large slice of cake and a glass of sherry, Isabel finally got a chance to talk to her granddaughter. 'Mia, it's been so long,' she said, embracing her. 'You're getting married?'

'I am. We haven't set a date yet but ... I'd love to get married here, at La Quida. If you agree, that is.'

'Here?' Isabel looked around at the ruins of her old home; the house she'd grown up in before the war.

'Yes. We could have a marquee and lights and it would be beautiful. As lovely as this party.'

'This is as much your place as mine; it's where our hearts and souls belong. Is he a good man? Do you love him?'

'Of course I do. Fernando is wonderful. He's a lawyer in Madrid.'

Isabel nodded. How times had changed. Her granddaughter was marrying a lawyer. The pride she felt almost brought tears to her eyes. Her granddaughter wouldn't have to starve.

'I haven't mentioned the wedding plans to mamá, as I only just thought of it.' Mia laughed. 'Don't mention it to her just yet, please.'

'No. I won't.'

'Yaya, have you met everyone here yet?'

'I don't know.' Isabel looked around the garden. 'I think so.'

'Wait here,' her granddaughter said, smiling as she left.

Isabel looked at the old stone house as she waited. The sun had shone on it and the clouds had rained on it and bullets had left their permanent marks on its walls. Still, in her eyes La Quida hadn't changed. Leaning on her cane she walked up to the large, sun-warmed stone that still stood by the remains of the kitchen wall. Her stone. Placing her cane against the wall she sat down and leaned back, closing her eyes and lifting her face towards the sun. A rainbow of colours through a sweet, papá's voice through the window, the sweet scent of rosemary carried from the hill on the wind. Memories she wished she had someone to share with.

'Mamá. Are you all right?' Mapi had appeared by her side.

Isabel opened her eyes and smiled. 'I am. Thank you for this.'

'There was another surprise, but we seemed to have lost him.'

'Him?'

'Yes. Tío Luis was here, but he's gone. I don't know if I should be worried.'

'Luis is here?' Isabel sat up and looked around. 'Let me try to find him.' She grabbed her cane with more energy than she'd had in years. *Now, where would he have gone?*

She walked along an overgrown path at the back of the house, towards a pine tree with low-hanging branches. He had to be there. Isabel was too old to get in there now herself but called out. 'Luis, this is my hiding place. You can't use it.'

Silence. She managed to move some branches out of the way, and on the damp mud sat her brother. He was old and had a bottle of sherry in his hand, but he was still her Luis. Her Luis who, somewhere along a hard and terrifying path, she'd lost. Somehow, Isabel managed to get into the hiding place but had no idea how she would ever get out again. She sat carefully down next her brother.

'This is my place, Luis. You should really have found one of your own.'

She brought up the past because it was the only thing they now had in common. Besides, hadn't she, just moments ago, wished she had someone to share her good memories? Here he was. The only one left.

'Happy birthday, Isabel,' Luis said, keeping his eyes on the bottle. 'It's been a long time.'

'You being here means the world to me, Luis. I thought I'd die without us having met again. I'm old now, you know.' Isabel attempted a laugh, but it fell short in the heavy atmosphere. Instead she took Luis's hand. 'How have you been?'

Her brother looked at her before his body shook and he started crying. Isabel put her arms around him, stroking his head until he calmed down. 'It's all going to be all right.'

'It won't,' he said, sitting back up, his hand still squeezing hers as tears streamed down his face. 'I'm sorry for everything. Everything.'

'You have nothing to be sorry about; I'm the one who let you down. You were my responsibility and I failed. You were so young, and I should have done better.'

'I know what happed. I don't blame you for running away. I did, once, but I know now you had your own problems....'

They sat in silence, content to leave those days in the past.

'Have you had a good life, Luis?' It mattered to her that he had been happy.

'I haven't had much to complain about. Happy? That's something I can't answer because I don't know how to. Until Pepe died a year ago I was all right. I looked after him, but he looked after me even more. You know, he would complain every day about my stubborn refusal to see or talk about you. Too much time had passed. The idea I couldn't contact you got so entrenched in my mind it was easier not to. When he died my life no longer had a purpose, and I started drinking more and more.' To emphasise this point, Luis took a swill out of the bottle. 'What about you? Have you been happy since we last met?'

'What's happy? We survived, and that's what matters. I have a daughter—a stubborn one at that—who is a journalist, and a granddaughter who is about to marry a lawyer—fancy that.' She paused. 'Do you remember when papá came home from his first posting to Málaga? When I was so envious of you being a boy, and therefore bound to be closer to papá than me, that I ran and hid in here. In this little place. Papá put his face through those branches and made everything all right. - That visit was the last one, and when he left we never saw him again. You know they're digging up papá's grave? At least they're digging where we think he's buried. Mapi is part of some organisation that conducts these digs all over the country. And, thanks to that, I had "Rojo" sprayed on my front door. Some things never change.'

'I have nowhere to live,' Luis blurted out. 'My house is being sold and I'm out on the street.'

Isabel was taken aback but soon recovered. 'You can always come and live with me. And La Quida may be in my name, but that was just so we could work the land. It's yours as well as mine and Mapi's and Mia's.'

'Great, I'll get a tent and pitch it here.... I'm sorry, I didn't mean it like that. It's just that everything has been a bit difficult since Pepe died. I let him down too, you know. Seems to be what I do best.' Luis took a large glug from the bottle.

Isabel sighed. Her little brother, the fisherman, the damaged little boy lost in the war, the drunk sitting next to her. 'You'll stay with me. You thought I let you down once, and I won't do it again. If I could stand up I would drag you back to the house now.' Isabel tried to get up. 'However, I think we're stuck here for a little while.'

'You won't try to run my life for me?'

'Why would I do that? I have enough problems running my own.' She smiled. 'Does that mean you're coming home?'

'I guess it does.' Luis stood up and then helped his sister. 'You're not as light as you once were.'

'I'll pretend I didn't hear that,' she said. He held the branches to one side and handed her the walking stick. 'I'm so glad you're here.'

The sun was now low in the sky, and the winter chill from the mountain had started to kick in as they walked slowly back to the party. Isabel felt complete. The emptiness that had nagged her most of her life had finally been filled. She had received Luis's forgiveness, and she would now be able to see her brother every day. Days and months and years were left to make him a good life, the life he should have had all along. She would spoil him, and he would no longer feel a need to drink to drown his sorrows. Arm in arm they walked along the path to find that the party had ended but the lights were still on. Mapi, Mia, and a few of Isabel's friends were cleaning up.

'There you are,' Mapi said, smiling. 'Lucky I saw you getting under that tree or I would have come looking for you earlier.'

'Thank you for the party. I'm sorry I missed the end.'

'That's all right. Most enjoyed themselves too much to notice the birthday girl's absence. It's getting chilly, so we should get you home.'

'I'll help clear up.'

'No, you won't. Besides, it's nearly done now.'

'Luis is staying with us for a while. We have the guest room, and you and Mia can share your bed.'

Mapi happily agreed. 'Let's just say goodbye and we can go.'

~ 10 ~

**Alicante, Spain
Spring 1939**

The lack of food was getting serious, and they would starve unless they got something to eat. So, shortly after they'd returned from church, Señora Alva and Isabel went searching for work. People had started moving around the city again, and the contrast between the soldiers and the civilian population couldn't have been stronger. Mostly women walked the streets, the men having been taken away. This left the women behind, as usual, to support the family and, a lot of the time, to send parcels of what food they could find to the prisons and camps where their husbands, fathers, sons, or daughters were held. There were rumours of overcrowding with no facilities, food, or water. Prisoners were dying by the thousands.

When they approached the market square where Señora Araya had died the previous year they were ushered down the street by the Guardia Civil, who then wouldn't let anybody back out.

Señora Alva turned to the woman next to her. 'What's going on?'

'There is another parade. They've be doing it all day. It's too awful to say out loud.'

The Guardia Civil walked around, guns in their hands, making sure everybody's attention was on the square.

A band stood in one corner of the square and in the middle were puddles of water, as if it had recently rained. The band started playing Nationalist songs and everybody had to join in. Then, from one of the streets leading into the square, shuffled five women. They were pushed forward and each tried to hide their nakedness as best they could.

'What's happening?' Isabel whispered, aghast. 'Who are they?'

'Some poor women being punished, that's who they are,' Señora Alva replied.

One of the guards nearby felt they were not paying enough attention to the spectacle in front of them and pointed his weapon at the women.

In the middle of the square now stood two stern-looking elderly women, both dressed in black. Isabel cold see their priest standing in the corner by the band, a smile on his lips. The naked women were forced onto their knees by the soldiers, and their long hair was shaved off by the women dressed in black.

Just when Isabel thought things couldn't get any worse, one of the elderly women, with the help of the soldiers, fed the captives liquid from a brown bottle. They coughed and gagged as it was forced down their throats.

'Castor oil,' said someone nearby. 'Those Rojos deserve it.'

Nobody dared argue with whoever had spoken, even though most of the city had been Republican or, as the person behind them preferred, "Rojos". Shortly after their comment the women in the square started bending over in pain, one after the other, as the castor oil started to work.

'Oh, Dios mio,' Señora Alva said, closing her eyes.

They were forced to stay in the square and watch the women clean up their mess before being ushered away. This was the worst punishment there could be, another act of terror to keep the population in check. To humiliate them.

They walked away in numb silence, but no matter how much they just wanted to go back home and forget the whole sorry day they couldn't. They had to find some food or they would starve. But the baker they always visited said there was no bread to be had at all; he wasn't even sure why he was made to open up his shop.

On their way out, they were stopped and searched for any unauthorised food stuffs, but as they had nothing they were let go. Two blocks down the road, the baker's son come running up behind.

'Señora, quick, take these.' He produced two loaves of bread from inside his jacket. 'My papá says it's to help your Pepe.'

Señora Alva took the bread and put in her basket under a cloth before anybody could see. 'Thank him so much. I'll be in to thank him myself tomorrow.'

'Don't worry about it. People will wonder where you got the bread if you don't go straight home. They might even steal it.' The boy ran back down the road from where he'd come.

Back home they ate the bread with some hot, watery soup and felt quite satisfied afterwards.

'I'd like to eat that every day,' Luis said, leaning back on the sofa with his hand on his stomach.

'Me too,' Pepe said, mimicking Luis's actions.

It had turned dark outside and even though nobody mentioned it, both Isabel and Señora Alva worried about from where their next meal would come. They didn't mention what had happened earlier in the square.

They decided that Isabel should go up to the hospital the following day to see if there was any cleaning or washing to be done. After all, she had past experience. Señora Alva would visit the big houses and try to get some cleaning work, which she'd done it in her youth before getting married.

They had just finished eating when there was a knock on the door and Señora Alva went to open it.

Outside stood the priest.

'Good evening, Señora Alva. Do you mind if I come in?'

'No, not at all. You're always welcome here.' She moved to let him past. 'I would offer you something to eat or drink, but I'm afraid we haven't got anything.'

The priest went over to the bed where Pepe lay. 'That's quite all right. I can smell that you've just eaten.'

Señora Alva smarted at the comment, and later told Isabel that she decided then, that whatever happened, there would be something to offer the next time he came around.

'I see now why this one doesn't come to church. What happened?'

Señora Alva walked up and stood next to Pepe. 'He lost his leg in a bombing raid, Father. He hasn't walked since.'

'He still has one leg, so he should, with assistance, be able to walk just up the road to church next Sunday.'

Señora Alva was silent for just a moment before agreeing. 'Of course. If you think that's best, that's what we'll do.'

'It's such a shame this episode in our history had to happen. So many people hurt, and even more of them led astray by those communists. Well, it's over now. I only came over to make sure you come to confession this week. If we are to move forward, you have to recognise your sins and mistakes, so you can do penance and be forgiven. That is, if you want God's forgiveness for your sins?'

'I do, Father. We all do.' She could have choked on the words, but the same old people, the same old government, and the same old church were back in power and she would bend over backwards and confess every sin they thought she'd ever committed if it saved her family from starving and the horrors they'd seen in the square.

'Well, I am glad to hear that. Now, I must leave. There are more of my old lambs to bring back to the fold. Until mass then, Señora.'

She showed him out and leaned against the door. Isabel knew this was the way it would be from now on. They needed to make sure there was always something to feed the priest during his visits.

The following morning, as they were washing up in the kitchen, they heard a commotion outside followed by a loud knock on the door. Everybody stopped and looked at each other in silence before another bang jolted Señora Alva into action. She took a deep breath and opened the front door.

Outside stood two Guardia Civil and the two black-robed women from the square; the same two who had shaved the women's hair the day before. Behind them stood the man from the window. All around their neighbours were being pulled from their houses and made to stand watch.

'Yes. Can I help you?' Señora Alva's eyes burnt into the senior Guardia Civil officer. There was no need to play the meek defeated woman any longer.

They pushed her back inside as the other Guardia Civil appeared in the kitchen where Isabel, Luis, and Señora Alva's old mother-in-law were standing as if frozen.

'We'll start with her.' One of the women pointed to Señora Alva. The Guardia Civil held her tight while the two women managed to undress her as she screamed abuse. The man from the window, the one Señora Alva had been convinced was a spy, started shaving her head.

Pepe shouted for them to stop and Luis cried loudly. Isabel heard their cries and Señora Alva's curses, but for her time had stopped. Maybe they would let her be; she'd done nothing wrong.

But the two women then moved towards Isabel and, knowing what was coming, she grabbed a knife from the table. It was small and blunt and no problem for the Guardia Civil who grabbed it from her. His hands grasped her arms so hard she cried out as much for that as to what was to come. All she could think was that Luis was watching. He would see her humiliation and things would never be the same.

'No!' She screamed at the top of her lungs. 'No!'

'Stand still, girl,' said one of the women as she tried to pull Isabel's arm from her dress. 'I can't get it off her. We'll have to cut it.'

The Guardia Civil let go of her arm and, taking the opportunity, Isabel ran out the kitchen door. She didn't know to where she would run, she just knew she had to get away. She had made it halfway up the stairs when someone grabbed one of her ankles and she fell. Her chin hit the step hard, but she didn't feel any pain. Isabel kicked her legs at the Guardia Civil as he dragged her back down and along the floor into the kitchen. She tried to get back up, but a blow from his truncheon sent a searing pain through her side and she fell back down. She could hear the others scream for him to stop as he kicked her back several times.

'Stop, now,' she heard one of the women say. 'We're holding everybody else up.'

The kicking stopped and the man pulled Isabel to her feet. 'Come on, stand up.'

The pain in her side and her back were so severe that even if she'd wanted to, Isabel wouldn't have been able to stand straight. The two women quickly cut off her dress and she wasn't able to do anything about it. She bent her head and closed her eyes. *Please make this stop. I'll do anything. Please.*

When the two women had removed her clothes, another approached and pulled her long brown hair loose from its plait. He cut it off in big chunks, leaving just a few centimetres on her head, which he the proceeded to shave off using only water and leaving long red marks along her scalp. Isabel cried now, though tried not to. *Keep calm, keep calm*, she thought, but couldn't. What had she done to deserve this? She couldn't look up at the rest of the crowded kitchen.

It took them only a few minutes to do the same to Señora Alva's old mother-in-law and then the Guardia Civil pushed them out onto the street. Some of their neighbours were in the same situation, including Paloma and her daughter-in-law from next door. A few houses down a military truck suddenly appeared, music blaring from its flat roof. Tinny Nationalist songs echoed down the street. Nobody made a fuss, knowing it would draw attention. Instead, they kept their eyes on the ground and hoped everybody else did the same.

The Guardia Civil in charge shouted instructions before they were pushed along. 'Now, you parade along after the van. You march, and you sing.' He paused as no one moved. 'Move and sing or I will personally kill every child in this street.' He pointed his gun at a little girl holding on to her mamá's skirts.

So they marched and sang the words praising a glorious Spain and the magnificence of its army. The words came out between burst of tears and panic as their neighbours and friends stood watching their humiliation.

Isabel tried to shut everything out. If she somehow survived, she would run away. Run to where this had never happened, somewhere, anywhere, else. Her eyes swelled with tears as she concentrated on the cobbles beneath her bare feet, trying to remove herself from what was happening. From what she knew was still to come.

Finally, they came to a halt in the middle of the square. The music didn't stop, but it wasn't loud enough to drown out the cries and gagging noises of the women. They all choked on the thick, oily liquid that was forced down their throats. Isabel screamed as loud as she could, losing all sense of what would have been the right thing to do. She screamed until they held her head back, opened her mouth, and pinched her nose before pouring the liquid down her throat. She couldn't breathe, and in a fit of panic she nearly blacked out.

Their hands had been tied behind their backs to avoid anyone sticking them down their throats and throwing the liquid back up. Once they had all been fed the castor oil the chairs on which they sat were removed and they were made to stand, still singing. The stomach pains started as a dull ache before turning into cramps then into excruciating pain. Isabel couldn't stop it, no matter how much she tried.

She didn't know for how long it went on, or how she managed, together with the others, to clean up the square afterwards.

Nobody looked each other in the eye. Heads were kept low, as if they had indeed done something wrong rather than being the victims of a brutal regime. After, they were paraded through the streets back the way they'd come.

Somewhere in that square Isabel had managed to detach herself from her body. She wasn't herself anymore, and she didn't know if she ever would be again.

Once their front door had closed behind them the three women washed themselves in the small courtyard. Their silence was complete.

When she was clean, Isabel sat in the courtyard wrapped in a blanket. Her stomach still hurt, and she couldn't bear the thought of being near any one of them again. She ran a hand over her sore, shaved head. Large blue and purple welts covered the right side of her stomach and, judging by the pain, her back too. She truly wished she'd died before this day, with mamá and her baby brother. Died with some dignity and without the knowledge that people, for no reason, would commit such crimes against other humans.

A few weeks earlier when, together with Irena, she had watched people in the harbour commit suicide before the fascists arrived by jumping into the sea, or shooting or stabbing themselves, she had felt so sorry for them. In reality they had been the lucky ones, the clever ones, the ones who knew what was coming and got out. Where were the rest of them now? Likely in prison camps either being worked to death or beaten to pieces. These were the thoughts that swirled around her mind as Isabel sat on a hard chair in the courtyard and stared into space. That and how she could leave this rotten city for good. She couldn't ask Luis to come along as for now he had a good home here. He could join her back home at the farm in good time.

After what had happened, she found it difficult to even think about Luis. She was supposed to look after him, she was supposed to be the strong one, the one in charge. But they had humiliated her and taken that away. It made her weak and ashamed. Isabel had to leave this place, but how could she when she knew she would never leave this house again?

***

For four days the household was in mourning. The only voices that could be heard were Luis and Pepe, talking quietly in the front room. During the daytime Isabel sat out in the courtyard, in a world of her own. The only thing she wanted was for it never to have happened. The Guardia Civil had cut her only dress so she now wore one of Señora Alva's, which was black and much too large for her skinny frame.

She'd tied a shawl over her itchy and stubby scalp, just as Señora Alva and mother-in-law had done. At night, when she was quite sure everybody was asleep, Isabel went inside to the front room and fell asleep, sitting up on the sofa. She'd had only a bit of water and some dry old bread to eat, which she had done only so they would again leave her alone.

It was on the fourth morning, when she'd gone back to her seat in the courtyard hoping to be left alone, that Señora Alva came out and stood awkwardly by the door. 'We shouldn't punish ourselves like this, Isabel. It wasn't our fault.'

Isabel glanced up before returning her gaze to the ground. She didn't want to talk to anybody about anything, especially not that.

Señora Alva took a step forward. 'We have to find something to eat. There are no more food parcels coming from the baker, and we'll starve to death if we don't do something. Are you listening to me? We all have to go out and see what we can find. There has to be something somewhere.'

Isabel again looked up. Was the woman serious? There was no way she was leaving this house until she was sure she'd be able to escape this town forever. She would rather starve. 'I can't go out. They all saw us, and they all know....'

'It's not a matter of being able to, Isabel, it's a matter of survival and, quite frankly, you need to pull your weight.' Tears had started to flow down Señora Alva's cheeks. 'I don't want to either. Everybody I know saw what happened, and when my husband finds out he will never look at me the same way again. As much as you can sit here feeling sorry for yourself, you're not the only one who's been injured. I won't have Pepe and Luis starve. If we don't go out and find some work or food, I'm going to have to send Luis out. He's old enough to help.'

Isabel stood up. 'No. You can't do that.' She didn't want him running around outside, where anything could happen. She couldn't bear it if she lost him, too.

'Yes, I can. I don't want to, but there's no other choice.'

Isabel slumped back down. 'All right. I'll go.'

'I knew you'd see sense. I'll go into town so you don't have to. You and mamá can go up to the hospital and see if they need any help. You might be lucky, some of the old hands might still be there. But stay away from Sister Magdalena; she always had a nasty streak and always took pleasure in handing out bad news. I'm sure she's fit in quite well with the fascists.'

'I'm not holding my breath. Who would employ me, with this badge of dishonour on my head?'

'There are people worse off than us, you know. We have to at least try to stay alive.'

It was nearly lunchtime when Isabel opened the door and stepped out into the sunshine. It was warm, but she felt as though it was mocking her by staying the same as it was before everything had happened. The road was almost empty, and she was glad they didn't live on one of the main roads through the city; she probably would never have left the house if so.

The house of Señora Alva's neighbour was dark, just as theirs had been. They still mourned for the dignity that had been taken away. She didn't think that Señora Alva had talked to her friend since it happened, and she wondered if this was how they all felt: all the women who'd been punished even though their only crime had been poverty and grabbing onto a ray of hope that Spain could be a country where everybody was free and given a chance in life. Since the parade she had hardly thought of anything but going back home to the village, a place not tainted....

Isabel's throat tightened as she stepped reluctantly out onto the cobblestones. Just behind her stood old Señora Fernandez, who almost had to push Isabel along the street. They could hear the mumbles of those they passed, judging them without knowing them. Their covered heads were all anyone needed to see to know what had happened.

Señora Fernandez walked along with her head held high, a defiant look in her eye, while Isabel stared at every cobblestone and mud patch along the way.

'Stop mooching, girl. They'll all think they're correct in judging us if you behave as if you're guilty.'

'They can see it on us anyway.' *Stupid old woman*, Isabel thought.

'What do you think our men have been through on the battlefields? What do you think they are going through right now? I can tell you it will be a hundred times worse than this. They'll get it out of their system, and in time it'll calm down. Head up now, girl.'

Isabel did as the old woman asked. People did stare; every single person they passed. Still, Señora Fernandez nodded and said 'hello' to everyone. Suddenly, Isabel couldn't decide whether she was too old to know better or if she had gone mad. Nobody returned her greetings, and people moved out of their way as if they had the plague. But that didn't stop some of them shouting abuse. Isabel realised she'd never really got to know the old woman and had always found her scary. In the beginning her beady little eyes had followed her around, making sure she didn't do anything wrong or steal whatever they had in the house. Now, Isabel felt a glimmer of respect. Señora Fernandez was right; they'd done nothing wrong, and even though she didn't join her in greeting the sneering strangers she held her head a little higher.

Still, their excursion was useless. Nobody would give them any work, and the staff at the hospital had been changed for Nationalist-friendly doctors and nurses who hadn't spent the war saving the lives of Rojos. If, by any chance, there was somebody there they knew, they would be ten times worse than the others just to prove their loyalty.

At the entrance to the hospital grounds they had been stopped by some guards. 'What do you want here?'

Señora Fernandez's flair for communication and pride had suddenly gone. There was a long period of silence before Isabel plucked up the courage to answer. 'We have only come to find some work, Señor.' In a mad moment she wasn't sure if she was supposed to curtsy.

This caused much laughter amongst the guards before they again turned serious. 'Do you think we'd let any sick person near the likes of you? They come here to get well, not catch some dirty infection. I should take you two down to the station to show you your lives are worth nothing. Now, get lost.'

Señora Fernandez thought it would be a good idea to try and get into the hospital from the back, but Isabel managed to convince her otherwise. Instead, the two women headed towards the countryside outside Alicante. As soon as they got away from the city the air smelled sweeter, and even though there were other people roaming the forest searching for food, for a little while Isabel felt almost normal.

The grass hadn't yet gone brown and dry, and she savoured the soft feel underneath her feet. She strolled across the grass, shoes in her hands, when she recognised a cluster of asparagus bushes. She gave them a couple of whacks with a stick to frighten away any snakes that may be hiding, and then started looking for the spears. She was rather disappointed when there were none in the first bush, but her mood improved as she found plenty underneath the second and third.

Along the way back she also found some wild garlic and onions. Isabel hid the food in her pockets and up her sleeves before going to find Señora Fernandez. She was waiting by the clearing and looked sternly at Isabel as she approached before breaking out in a wide smile. Her pockets were full of red berries. Some had even started to leave mushy red stains.

'I don't understand why nobody else has found this place. Half the town must be roaming around trying to find food, yet here we are with all this,' said Señora Fernandez as they started walking back to the house. 'I think it's very important we keep this a secret.'

Isabel agreed and they started walking as quickly as possible, both with their heads down as to not attract attention to themselves or to their hoard.

They found Señora Alva in the kitchen preparing sardines. 'Did you find any work at the hospital? You've been gone a long time.'

'No, but we found this.' Isabel and Señora Fernandez emptied their pockets onto the table.

'I haven't even seen this kind of food since the early days of the war,' said Señora Alva, and she started to prepare the dinner.

'Where did you get the sardines from?' Isabel asked.

'Now, don't get mad.' She looked at Isabel. 'They were payment for some work Luis did for one of the fishermen down on the beach.'

Isabel gaze bored into hers. 'You promised. You promised he wouldn't have to go out if I went up to the hospital. I only did it to save him from the awful people of this horrible town.'

'Say what you like, but it was only for a few hours and he enjoyed it. Didn't you, Luis?'

Isabel turned to look see him standing in the doorway, nodding in response.

'And you're doing it again tomorrow, aren't you?'

'I am. The fisherman told me lots of stories while I fixed his nets. He was with the other side in the war, so I kept quiet about ours.'

'You shouldn't have let him go,' Isabel said before going back out to the courtyard and her usual spot. But she didn't stay angry very long as the smell of frying fish wafted through the partly open door. She needed food.

They ate the fired fish with the onion and asparagus, along with plenty of garlic. The fish heads and bones were boiled to make stock for the soup they would have the following day. The whole house smelled of food, just like the good old days. When Isabel went to bed that night she felt a small light at the end of the tunnel, feeling that maybe, at some point, everything would all right.

Señora Fernandez and Isabel didn't go back to the field the following day, as they didn't want to attract attention to their little find. Again they ate sardines in the evening and, even though there was still an odd strain between Luis and Isabel, they all felt a little brighter than they had for some time.

The next day Isabel and Señora Fernandez gathered more asparagus, but it was getting late in the season and it was starting to show. Even so, they had a good amount of food in their pockets and they started walking back home.

Isabel was so intent on keeping her eyes on the road that she nearly bumped into one of the soldiers roaming the streets of Alicante. Their look of recognition was instant.

'I've been looking for you,' said the soldier who had tried to drag her into the alleyway. 'I believe you still have some outstanding charges.'

Isabel's eyes flickered around for an escape route, finding none. There were three of them now and she had nowhere to run. 'You have me confused with someone else. I've never met you. We're just on our way home.' She looked around, but Señora Fernandez had disappeared. *Keep calm, Isabel. Whatever happens, just keep calm.*

'It's a nasty habit to lie. Especially to us, Rojo.'

Before she realised what was happening, they'd grabbed hold of her and thrown her onto the floor of the covered truck.

It was almost a week before they threw her out, bruised and unconscious, in the same place they'd picked her up.

***

It was dark when her eyes flickered open. The straw mattress on which she lay on smelled damp, and the blanket covering her itched. Isabel didn't move. There was a certain calm in the darkness she didn't want to disturb. She didn't know how she got where she was, or how long she'd been there, and she didn't know if they would come back. With her next breath came a deep sob. It nearly choked her, and she pulled the blanket over her face to keep the sound from attracting attention. Her whole body shook and she bit her lips to try and stop her cries, to no avail.

Through the fog she heard movement as soft footsteps approached.

'Isabel, are you awake?' A woman put her hand on top of the shaking bundle under the blanket. 'It's all right now. You're safe. I promise.' The woman pulled the blanket from her face and lay down beside Isabel. She pulled the girl to her, holding her until she calmed down.

'The bastards. Don't you worry, they'll pay for this.' Irena whispered into the night. 'One day, they will pay for it all.'

When the light of dawn drifted in through the broken window, Irena made them tea. They drank in silence by the window, where the sound of softly moving waves mixed with traders starting their day's business. Irena's room was on the third floor, a little farther away from the town centre than the one they'd shared earlier.

Isabel couldn't bear the questions she knew would come. She wouldn't be able to answer them. The horror of what had happened made the parade pale in insignificance. She had been sure that was where she would die—that's what they'd told her—and that was for what she'd hoped. Yet against all odds she lived. Each day she had survived in that truck they cut her arm with a knife. Five lines on the top of her arm; they'd not bothered on the sixth. Now they were scabbed and hard, and part of who she was.

Isabel needn't have worried about Irena asking any questions; she knew better than that. She knew what happened without needing it confirmed by words.

She handed Isabel a bun topped with little round lumps of sugar. 'I saved it for you, Bella. Thought you might like it.'

Isabel tried to smile but found it impossible. 'Thank you.' She took a small mouthful. It was difficult to open her mouth too much, as the cuts and bruises on her face hurt when she did. Even the hot tea hurt too much to drink, so she had to leave it until it cooled down.

Isabel looked at her friend. 'Where did they take you?'

'Down to the police station, and then to prison. They tried to get names from me any way they could. All unpleasant and painful, but I gave them nothing.'

'How come they let you go? I thought they'd keep you there forever.'

Irena gave a hollow laugh. 'Because I bribed them in the end. Took every penny I'd saved since I started working, well, like I do now. It was worth it. If I'd survived in the prison until my trial they would have sent me away to some camp for the rest of my life and a day, and that would have been it. All for belonging to a particular political party.' She smiled and gently squeezed Isabel's knee. 'So now I have to save up again, Bella. We'll save our pennies and leave this hole of a city. We can both go home.'

Isabel shut her eyes. 'Do you know how Luis is? And Señora Alva?'

'Don't you worry about him, Bella. Señora Alva was bragging about the sardines he brings home, and he looked happy when I saw him last. He knows nothing of what happened.'

Irena lit a cigarette and took a deep drag before handing it to Isabel. After a second's hesitation she accepted. She felt the smoke enter her lungs and as she blew out she felt calmer.

'Did they tell you what happened?' She touched her head, where almost a centimetre of soft brown hair had appeared.

'I didn't need telling. When I went to see if you were still there, Señora Alva just nodded when she saw me looking at her head scarf. She did tell me you'd been arrested, but when I went down to the police station there was no record of it at all. Then I went back to the house, and that's when some woman came knocking on the door to tell us you'd been found unconscious just up the road. We rushed over and managed to get you back to the house. You did wake up for the walk, but obviously can't remember. Then we decided it would be better for you to come here and stay with me, at least for the time being. You don't mind, do you?'

Isabel didn't care wherever she lived, as long as it wasn't in that truck. The sun played on the sea and couples walked hand in hand alongside the promenade. What had they done to deserve to be so happy when so many others were miserable?

'You know we have to be stronger than them, Bella. You see what they've done to us, to this country and our families. They might have better weapons and more powerful friends, but they will never break our spirit. One day we'll beat them back, show them the same mercy in defeat as they've shown us. Those you see out walking are all fascists; the ones cowering in the corners starving to death are the people whose government was overthrown and on who the world's governments turned their backs. They had recognised Franco's government before he'd even won the war. And the Republican government here was the most useless government anywhere else in the world; a cowardly one at that.

'You know what? I found out all the people we saw on the beach, hoping for boats to come and take them away to safety, were left there as fascist fodder and just up the road were boats collecting the government and their officials. They ran away and left us here to be punished for their incompetence.'

Isabel was no longer awake to see Irena look over after getting so wrapped up in her speech. She'd fallen asleep with her head against the wall, the blanket still wrapped around her, and the sugary bun only tasted. When she woke she'd find Irena had rewrapped the bun, ready to eat.

It was still early in the morning and as Isabel slept, Irena, with demons of her own to keep at bay, reached behind the sack she used as a pillow and pulled out a bottle of wine. She would have bought something stronger if she could.

When Isabel woke maybe Irena would tell her that in a few months' time she would probably have saved enough money for them both to go back to Málaga, for Isabel and Luis to go back home.

***

It was mid-summer before Isabel dared venture outside again. Her hair was short, but it suited her small face. Even though she still wore a scarf, like a Moorish woman, she no longer minded taking it off at home. Her hatred for the fascists grew every evening over the wine and cigarettes she consumed by herself at the window while Irena worked in the next room. Every evening she silently cried until there were no more tears left.

She'd once again got used to Irena's work, but now Isabel felt guilty for eating her food and staying in her flat without contributing. So she decided to start working for herself. She too would need money to go home, and then, when everything had settled down and Franco felt safe and secure, she'd join the uprising and take pleasure in ripping open the throats of every fascist bastard she saw.

Every morning, however, as the fog of alcohol lifted Isabel grew nervous and edgy, expecting someone to burst in and again take either herself or Irena away. She usually woke with a headache and an upset stomach, which didn't clear until noon; around the same time Irena rose. She was the only person in the world Isabel thought understood what had happened to her, the only one in the world with whom she didn't feel embarrassed just being around. What would have happened if Irena hadn't managed to get out of prison? The money she'd spent on bribes had saved them both.

Two and a half years earlier, when Isabel had arrived in Málaga with mamá and Luis, when Irena had let them into Señora Araya's house for the first time, she'd never expected to become friends with the brash grown-up who obviously didn't like her. Maybe they'd simply become friends because of what they'd been through, or maybe because, apart from Luis, they were the only two left alive.

For weeks Isabel told herself she'd go see her brother the following day. It had been a long time since she'd seen him last, but with every day that passed it became more difficult to go. She knew if she didn't go soon, she might lose Luis forever.

One day, Isabel made up her mind. 'I want some of the work you do,' she said to Irena that afternoon as they sat by the window, looking out over a cloudy sea.

'I don't think so. You can't undo it once you start. It'll be with you forever.'

'I know, but I want to make some money to get home and maybe give a little to Señora Alva for looking after Luis.'

'Most of them only pay in bits of food or wine, but there are some who have money now.'

'Perhaps I could give Señora Alva some of the food or wine.'

'Bella, stop it. Most of us barely make enough to stop ourselves from starving. I've been lucky and make more than most. Got a few tricks up my sleeve.'

'What tricks?'

'I'm not going to tell you. I really don't think it's something you should do, Bella. Despite everything that's happened I still hope you'll have a good life away from all this. If you go down my route it'll be more difficult for you to leave it behind. I'll make us a little bit of money, and maybe we'll go next summer.'

'If I help too, we can go earlier. I hate this town.'

'We'll talk about it another time.'

Isabel looked out the window and onto the sea. Anywhere would be better than here.

When Isabel ventured from the flat, she noticed changes everywhere. Families were left starving on the streets, begging passersby for any scraps they could get. Men, women, and children were thin like rakes, and had a glazed look to their eyes. They were the beaten, and their fortune could so easily have been that of her and Luis. But she shouldn't tempt fate; she hadn't seen Luis or the others for ages and they might now be starving too.

Stepping outside the front door had been one of the bravest things Isabel had ever had to do; she expected the whole town to know what had happened. Yet what she found was a population too busy keeping itself alive to care about others. As she reached Señora Alva's street she had to push herself forward. Nothing good had happened to her here, and with every step her heart rate increased. When she finally reached the house, the door was opened by an old woman she'd never seen before. She was dressed in black rags and her grey hair was tied back in a bun.

'Si,' said the old woman sharply while looking baldly at the shawl covering Isabel's head.

'Is Señora Alva here?' Isabel asked her.

'No. They moved. I don't know where they've gone, and I don't want to know,' said the old woman as she moved back to close the door.

Isabel would have put her foot in the doorway to stop her closing it, but she had no shoes. Instead, she pushed it open with her hands. 'What do you mean they've moved?' Her voice was now shrill with worry. Had the fascists got them, too?

'I don't know. They just left, and I moved in. That's all there is to it. Don't you go around causing problems. I found the house and the woman said I could have it.' She pushed the door shut and this time Isabel let her.

She stood for a moment staring at her old front door before knocking on the neighbour's. 'Señora Puerta, I've just come to visit Señora Alva and my brother, but they seem to have gone.'

Señora Puerta looked around before ushering Isabel inside. In all the time she'd lived next door she'd never seen the inside of the house and found it looked remarkably similar to Señora Alva's. Señora Puerta also wore a shawl around her head to cover the short hair Isabel assumed must be growing back.

'They left about two weeks ago. She tried to find you, but she didn't know where that woman lived. She wasn't even sure you were alive.'

'Oh, I should have come earlier.' She'd spent too long wallowing in self-pity, and now they were gone.

'Well, yes, you should have, but after everything that's happened, I don't suppose anybody can blame you.'

Isabel put her head in her hands but didn't start crying. She was done with that and instead looked back up. 'Do you know where they've gone?'

'Yes. Señora Alva got a message saying her husband was being held in a camp outside Barcelona, and so she packed up their things and left. That old woman who has moved into the house didn't waste any time. She's not even from this area; she's from some village on the other side of the country. I think she managed to escape the round-ups after the fascists came and now she's decided to stay. What will happen when Señora Alva comes back, I don't know.'

Isabel had no idea where Barcelona was, so she asked.

'It's up north. Not too far from here, but I don't know exactly where.'

'What about Pepe? How did he leave?'

'He had started walking with the help of a stick, and some help from your brother.'

Isabel nodded and got up from the chair in which she'd been sitting. 'Thank you, Señora.'

Paloma stood and looked at Isabel's stomach. 'You're pregnant.' It was a statement, not a question.

Isabel jolted. 'No. Why would you say that?'

'My dear girl. I've delivered babies for more than forty years and I know a pregnant woman when I see one.'

'Well, I'm not. How could I be?' Isabel went back to the front door and stepped out onto the street, but Señora Puerta followed her outside.

'Remember, if you need any help send a message. I'll come.'

Isabel walked away, asking herself why Señora Puerta would want to upset her so.

***

Over the following months she tried to put Señora Puerta's words out of her mind but found it impossible. Visions of her mamá giving birth on the hillside, while shells were exploded everywhere, appeared when Isabel closed her eyes. The pain she'd been in, and how it had killed her, scared her almost as much as letting anybody know.

Autumn came and Señora Alva and Luis still hadn't returned. Isabel couldn't go and find them now, not in the situation she was in. If anybody found out she'd be put in prison or a convent for being pregnant and unmarried. Nobody would care how it had happened. She was sixteen years old.

'You should try to get some work somewhere, Bella. Your hair is looking fine now, and you have to leave this flat sometime. It's not healthy for you to stay in all the time.' Irena repeated these sentences almost daily, and Isabel had started to dread them. Every time she agreed with her, saying she'd do it later in the week when she felt a little better.

When Irena walked in on her changing her clothes Isabel knew her secret was out.

'Why didn't you tell me?'

Isabel stayed quiet, not knowing what to say.

'If you'd told me earlier we could have done something about it. Now what are we going to do?'

'I'm sorry, I didn't know at first and then I hoped it would go away on its own.'

She put on her dress and went over to the window. It was cloudy and a chilly wind blew from the north. 'I don't want to keep it. I don't want to give birth, either.'

'I don't think we have that much of a choice. So, that's why you haven't gone out. I thought it was still your nerves.' Irena stayed still. 'I guess it must be six months by now,' she said, looking at Isabel's stomach. 'Which means it will be due in January. You're going to have to have it, and then we'll hand it over to the church or something. Poor bloody child.'

'I can't do it, Irena. I really can't.'

'Of course you can. What do you think women have done since the dawn of time? It's not ideal, but it won't stop us travelling to Málaga in the spring, will it?'

Isabel shook her head. 'No, it won't. Unless I die.'

'It would be better if we could go somewhere in the countryside or into the mountains for the birth. If anyone hears anything we'll have every Guardia Civil in town at our door. Damn their unjust bloody morals.' She looked around and picked up her cigarettes. 'I have to go, Bella. Try not to worry about it too much. What's done is done and we'll just have to deal with it.'

She left the room and Isabel sat down on the bed, knowing she couldn't go through with the pregnancy or the birth.

Christmas came and went, and so did January. All Isabel did was pace around the room like some mad animal. It wasn't until the middle of February, a week before her seventeenth birthday, that she started getting painful cramps. They came and went, and thanks to Irena's earlier words of wisdom, she knew the baby wanted to come out. She sat down on the floor, her eyes screwed up tight against the bursts of pain. Irena was out working. She had taken it upon herself to pop back every couple of hours to make sure Isabel was all right, so she'd be back soon.

Isabel had managed to convince herself something would go wrong, that she wouldn't see another day once it started. She tried to concentrate on something else, like the escape from this hellhole of a town they were planning regularly. She tried to imagine the house where she'd grown up and could see it clear as day. The sun was shining, and she was sitting on her stone with the sweet Señor Enrique Chavez always gave her. It was calm, the sun warm on her skin, and the sound of mamá washing clothes at the back blended into the landscape. papá came walking down the path from the village; he smiled, and she smiled back.

Behind him was Señor Chavez, Antonio, and Pilar, all smiling. Pilar wore a normal dress, not the men's militia clothes she'd seen her in the day before they left. She wondered briefly where Pilar was now the war had been lost. Maybe she'd gone back home, or maybe she was with her new husband. She could even have children by now. Another shock of pain tore through Isabel, shattering the illusion.

When Irena stopped by to see if she was all right, she found her friend curled up on the mattress and rushed over. 'How long has it been going?'

'I don't know. A while.' Isabel only answered when there was a pause in the pain. 'You have to get Señora Puerta. She said she'd help. Quickly.'

Irena looked doubtful. She'd never got on with Señora Puerta. Isabel knew there were many reasons they disliked each other but the main one, the one Irena had never forgiven, was that she'd told Señora Alva she was a prostitute. Never mind how true that actually was. 'Are you sure she's not going to tell anyone?'

'Just go, or I will die right here.' Isabel again curled up against the pain.

For a moment Irena hesitated, then made up her mind. 'Right. I'll be as quick as I can,' she said, rushing out the door.

The pains were getting worse and worse, and Isabel tried her best not to shout. They didn't want the neighbours to know what was going on. Only herself, Irena, and Señora Puerta knew about the baby and that's the way it would have to stay. How much longer would it go on? She tried once again to recall the house and the happy memories she knew were there, but she couldn't. The pain was just too much. She cursed silently, like she'd heard the soldiers on the road to Almería do and wondered if she'd have time to take a couple of drags of a cigarette in between the contractions. She decided against it. They didn't have any alcohol, but if they did, she would have drunk it all to try and numb the pain that was tearing her apart. It must be over soon; she couldn't take any more.

It felt as though a lifetime passed before Señora Puerta strode into the room behind Irena.

'It smells in here. It's not very feminine to smoke.' She glared briefly at Irena before turning her attention to Isabel. 'Now, how are we doing here?'

Hours passed, and Isabel lost the will to live. She no longer cared what happened to her, as long as the pain stopped.

'Not long now,' Señora Puerta said calmly. 'There we go, I can see the head.' A few minutes later she had cleaned the baby up and wrapped it in an old scarf. 'It's best if we go,' she said. 'You don't want to upset yourself by seeing the baby.'

Isabel looked at the bundle in Señora Puerta's arms and found she didn't care one bit. The only thing she felt was an overwhelming sense of relief it was all over. 'Is it a boy or a girl?'

Señora Puerta shook her head. 'It's best you don't know. It doesn't matter, does it?'

'No, I suppose it doesn't matter at all.' Isabel turned away to go to sleep.

She could hear them whispering by the door before Señora Puerta left with the baby. She was supposed to leave it at the church or, if that wasn't possible, she'd say she found it on the street and hand it over to the priest.

Isabel was so very tired, but she couldn't sleep. There was nothing she wanted more, but it wouldn't come. She kept picturing mamá's birth and the affection she'd shown for the baby, even though she must have known she was dying. Even in that situation, with everything going on, she had still wanted her new boy to be looked after. Yet Isabel had managed to get rid of that responsibility, too, and although she knew it wasn't her fault he'd died, she knew she should have found something to feed him. And now she'd lost Luis. Why was she being punished like this?

There was a noise by her bed, and she turned around. Her papá sat by her side and put his hand on her cheek. Tears of joy and relief started to flow, but she couldn't move. She wanted to hold him and tell him how she'd missed him, but no words came from her lips. He just touched her face and sat looking at her, sadness in his eyes. His white shirt was stained with blood and dirt. 'I'm sorry,' he seemed to say, and she knew then that he had died.

Irena woke her up with tea and a sugary bun. Isabel had no idea where she got them, but they appeared from time to time, when she felt as though Isabel needed them.

'How are you feeling? You've slept for a long time.'

Isabel just lay there, the tea and bun untouched by her side.

'You should eat. The sugar will give you energy and you won't believe what I had to do to get it for you.'

Isabel looked up at her. 'He's dead.'

'No, he isn't. Señora Puerta watched the priest find him, and he's being looked after just fine somewhere.'

'No. papá. I saw him last night.' Isabel turned over. She couldn't bear the thought. That her baby had been a boy didn't register.

'It was just a dream, Bella. You were tired after everything that happened yesterday and you had some strange dreams, that's all. Don't think they're real. We know better than that.'

Isabel ignored her; she hadn't seen him. He had been as real as he'd ever been.

'Come on. Drink your tea and eat the bun, or I'll have to stay here forever to make sure you do.'

Isabel sat up, grimacing with pain as she did so. She had formed a plan, and she needed to leave the house to complete it. She ate the bun and drank the tea, and when Irena brought home a couple of sardines later that day, she ate them too. She tried walking around the flat but doing so was painful and she'd been told to stay still so she'd have the best chance of healing.

Still, Isabel didn't need it to last long, and all she wanted to do was to get down to the beach. If she started to bleed there it wouldn't matter. In fact, it might help the process. For a moment she felt guilty at leaving Irena in such a way. She had been the best friend anyone could possibly have, and she wished she could tell her that, but of course she couldn't because that would alert her to Isabel's plan.

When she closed her eyes, she could still see papá sitting by her bedside. She hated his sad look, and tried to replace it with the sparkly grin he wore whenever she went to meet him at the crossroads; when he'd lift her up and tell her how mamá would be upset with her for not staying at the house, working like she should be. She thought about how much he'd loved the asparagus she found, and how she kept hunting for them just to see him smile. Why did those days have to disappear? She didn't ask for riches or beauty, all she wanted was her family back again. They couldn't come to her, so she'd have to go to them.

Irena had gone out to see if she could find some food. They'd been running low, as Isabel had tried to eat everything in sight to get enough strength for her mission. She dressed in the only dress she had, combed her hair, which now came down to her shoulders, and took one last look around the little room she'd left only a handful of times.

If she wished for anything it was that she could leave Luis a message, give him a reason why she had done what she had to do. Irena would understand. She'd seen her worried glances when she thought Isabel wasn't looking. She wanted Irena to know she would never have got this far without her help, and wished she had something to leave her friend. She wanted to give assurance she didn't do it because of her lack of attention, but that she had to do it because she couldn't bear to live any more.

Isabel stepped outside the door, went down the stairs, and walked out onto the street. People walked along, to or from work, and there were beggars everywhere. Soldiers and the Guardia Civil watched for mischief. She didn't want to be spotted by Irena or stopped by anybody else before she'd done what she wanted to do, so she walked along the promenade. When she reached the quieter part of town she turned onto the cold, sandy beach. It was deserted, as was to be expected that time of the year. The wind, which had been blowing hard all day, had now calmed down a little. She walked towards the sea, no longer caring if anybody saw. They'd just think she was about to dip in her toes to see how cold it was.

The icy water covered her bare feet as they sank into the sand. Isabel started to walk further out, keeping her eyes on the horizon. She was a mountain girl and didn't know how to swim; it would be quite a quick death. Her teeth chattered as she felt the water creep ever higher, her feet growing numb with the cold. Every inch she walked chilled her to the bone, but she enjoyed it because it was her choice and not that of someone else. How would she get far enough out to properly drown?

She stood on her tiptoes and pulled up her legs up to force her head under the water. Her back floated up and the panic set in. Isabel started flailing her arms to regain her balance, but her feet no longer reached the bottom. She fought on for as long as she could, but it was inevitable she'd go under the surface.

***

Isabel had been so intent on her task she hadn't heard the man behind her. He'd waded towards her through the water, and as her head started to go under the surface he had reached out and pulled her onto the beach.

'You stupid girl, why would you do that?'

She was lying on the beach, coughing up seawater.

'People everywhere are fighting to stay alive, and you want to kill yourself? If someone else had found you they would have sent you to prison. Maybe you'd have got the death sentence; ironic, isn't it?'

Isabel simply laid on the sand. The last drops of ocean had been expelled from her lungs and she shook in the cold air. Her hair was wet and clung to her face. Why, why, why hadn't it worked? She hadn't realised her body would float upwards. She thought that if she'd kept on walking the water would rise over her head and she would just disappear under the surface. It would be quick. What would she do now?

The man was still there. 'Do you have anywhere to go?'

Who did he think he was? If he'd left her there, she'd be with her family now. Abruptly she sat up. 'What gives you the right to interfere? You should stay out of things that don't concern you. You should just have left me there.'

He laughed. 'I should have done, shouldn't I? I'm all cold and wet, and I know if you want to do it again you will.' He stood up. 'Do you want me to walk you back to where you live?'

Isabel shook her head and stared at the sand in front of her. Out of the corner of her eye she watched him leave. She picked up some of the cold sand and let it slip back onto the beach through her fingers.

A pair of Guardia Civil boots appeared beside her. 'Stand up.'

She scrambled to her feet. He was on his own.

'What are you doing here? It's February.' The policeman looked at Isabel's wet hair and clothes. 'Did someone push you into the water?'

Isabel could still see the back of the man who'd helped her, and if she ran she could reach him. She refused to let them get her again and so she spun around and started running, kicking up sand as she went. *Run, Isabel; faster, faster.* She didn't know where the Guardia Civil was until she felt his hand grab her arm and pull her to a stop. The man in front, the one who had rescued her from the water had turned around when he heard her shout, but he'd very quickly turned back and increased his speed to get away from the guard. He didn't want the trouble; he probably had enough of his own.

'Running away from a Guardia Civil is punishable by law. Why were you trying to escape?'

She still said nothing.

'Answer me, or I'll take you to the station.'

He kept asking her questions for a little while, but Isabel didn't hear him. She'd put up her protective walls, where his voice didn't reach.

In a dreamlike state she allowed herself to be pulled along the streets of Alicante to the police station. They pushed her into a cell so full of women she could hardly fit and only then, when she knew she was in the company of others like herself, did she start to relax.

As there was hardly room to stand there was no room to sit down. As awful as that place must have seemed to most, Isabel could have cried with relief there wasn't a repeat of the brutality of the last time she was caught. It smelled so bad she tried to breathe through her mouth, if only to stop her from gagging.

One of the women further down the cell shouted at the newcomer. 'What are you here for?'

'I don't know.' Isabel answered quietly.

'Speak up. We can't hear you down here.'

'She said she doesn't know why she's here,' shouted one of the women closer to Isabel. 'I'm Gabriela,' she said. 'I'm here for fighting for freedom.' She was a short woman in her twenties, with green eyes and long brown hair plaited down her back.

'I panicked and ran away from a Guardia Civil,' Isabel said.

'Well, I can certainly understand why you'd want to run, but they seem to take themselves very seriously.'

'What are you talking about over there?' It was the first woman who'd shouted. 'Hold on, I'm pushing through.'

There were many grumpy comments as whoever this woman was made her way towards Isabel and Gabriela.

'So, why are you here? What's your name and where are you from?'

Gabriela stared at the woman. 'She's not being interrogated here, Maria.'

'I'm sorry, I just wanted to know. Maybe she knows someone I know.'

'I'm Isabel. I'm from a village north of Málaga.'

'Ah, I don't know anyone down south.'

'She asks everyone,' Gabriela said.

'I need to get a message to my husband, but I don't know where he is and he won't know where I am. I just thought that if I let enough people know then maybe, if they get out before me, they could find him and tell him.' Maria shrugged her shoulders and went back to the place from where she'd come.

There must have been over forty of them squeezed into the cell, and there was no way they could fit anybody else.

Isabel's conversation with Gabriela fizzled out and the reality of where she had ended up started to creep in. At first she'd been relieved she'd been taken to the station, but now she worried about how she'd get out. They couldn't hold her, surely; she'd done nothing wrong. Nothing they knew of, anyway. But as she hadn't listened to what they were saying as she was brought in she didn't know for sure. She recalled them asking her name and details, but her head had still been foggy from the panic attack on the beach. She could tell them now but she didn't want to attract attention to herself, so she stayed standing where they had pushed her in.

Through the long day and night, the women took it in turns to lie down on the floor, and at regular intervals they were collected for interrogation. When they came back, they usually looked worse for wear, and so were allowed a spot on one of the sleeping mats to rest.

It was another full day before they came to collect Isabel. As they didn't know her name, they simply called her Rojo. She found that rather funny, as most of them there were Rojos. Gabriela squeezed her arm in reassurance before she left.

The corridor was badly lit and had a sour smell about it. As it wasn't a large police station they didn't have far to go. Isabel sat down on a chair and the questions started.

This time she did tell them her name and where she was from, where her family was, and what they had been doing during the war. She said she didn't know what her papá had done, but when they asked if he had been part of a union, which would have meant fighting in some way against the Franco forces, she said yes. Her father had belonged to the CNT union, and because she'd told them that already she couldn't take it back. Then came the questions about other people in her village: who else had belonged to the union, did she know any crimes they committed? To all these questions she said she didn't know the answer. She said she had only been a girl at the time and her papá never spoke about it at home. She would never tell them about Enrique, Antonio, Pilar, or all the others. That was the one thing Isabel swore she would never tell them, no matter what they did to her. She wished she'd kept quiet about her papá too, but that day, when they came and arrested Irena, she didn't realise just how bad things were going to get.

Every time Isabel didn't give the answers they wanted, one of the uniformed men hit her with a baton before asking again. This was repeated throughout the afternoon, and when that man lifted his baton and brought it down onto her arms or into her stomach, she hoped it would be the last one.

When they led her back into the cell, she was doubled over. She was bleeding, and there was a pain inside her that cut like sharp knives every time she moved. Maybe something hadn't healed up from the birth, or maybe they had just broken her; whatever it was she was given a priority space on the floor. The other women told her to stay there until the bleeding stopped. But even lying down on the cold hard floor hurt so much Isabel would rather have stood, she just didn't have the energy. Maybe her plan would still work; she would die here, a prisoner, filthy and in pain, instead of in a place of her own choosing.

The woman who'd first asked her where she was from hunched down next to her. Her name was Maria, like Isabel's mamá. 'Stay strong,' she whispered. 'We've still got a whole war to fight. We'll get through this.'

Later, when the bleeding had finally stopped and Isabel had slept for a while, she stood up and leaned against a wall. Maria told her about her war, about the places she'd been and the friends she'd lost. One thing she hadn't lost was her beliefs and ideals; too many had died for those ideals to give up now. 'The mistake I made was going home. Everybody knew where I'd been, but there was nowhere else for me to go.'

'What do you think will happen to you now?'

'I don't know. They seem to kill a lot of people for very little reason, but you never know. I might just get a prison sentence. I only wish I knew where Amando, my husband, is. If you get out, will you try to find him and tell him where I am?'

'Of course I will.' Isabel didn't quite understand why she'd agreed because she had enough to deal with herself. Yet the look on Maria's face when she agreed to try and find him was one of pure relief.

'You'll get out. You haven't been involved in anything illegal.'

'They kept asking me for names of people in my village who were part of my papá's union.'

'Don't tell them anything. They'll get them anyway, but let's not make it easier for them.'

They didn't collect Isabel for another interrogation. The next time they came it was to take her and another twenty of the women to court. Both Maria and Gabriela were included and joined Isabel as they were put in a long line and marched out and into a waiting truck.

At the courthouse they were herded into a line in front of a judge. There was one lawyer to deal with all their cases, and he had no information as to any of the prisoners' defence. All he had were the files he'd been given by the prosecution half an hour before.

Gabriela's parents waited in the public area, but she wasn't even allowed to look at them. Nobody was there for Isabel, but she hadn't expected there to be. After all, she now had no one apart from Irena, who she'd treated so terribly by leaving.

The women stood next to each other as their charges were read in quick succession. It was then Isabel found out she'd been charged with trying to escape arrest. The defence lawyer had nothing to say on anyone's behalf, so the judge read out their sentences without even looking at the people whose lives he held in his hands.

Out of twenty women, two were handed death sentences and eighteen handed prison sentences varying between two years and a day to twenty-five years and a day.

Isabel got lucky, receiving the lowest prison term. Gabriela was sentenced to fifteen years and a day; Maria was sentenced to death.

When Maria heard the judge say her fate out loud her legs buckled, and she collapsed to the floor. Isabel was sure her new friend would have died for her beliefs with pride, but the thought of never seeing her husband again proved too much. Gabriela and Isabel pulled her back up while the judge looked on with disgust.

'I take no pleasure in handing out the harshest of sentences to women, but you lot are no longer women in the eyes of the law—if you ever were.' He rose from his chair as guards came to lead them away.

Outside the courthouse the women were split into two groups. Isabel found herself in an army truck with five other prisoners, including Gabriela and Maria. The six women sat on single wooden bench, while in the seats opposite sat two bored soldiers. The truck smelled of petrol and metal and the brakes screeched.

Maria had stopped crying, but Isabel and Gabriela kept her between them, arms linked in solidarity. Nobody knew where they were going but figured it might be quite some distance, as when they got off the truck, they joined still more prisoners at a railway station outside Alicante. All in all, twenty women huddled together against the cold evening air. After several hours of waiting by the tracks, a train finally slowed to a stop and they were herded into an already full carriage.

'Does anybody know where we're going?' Gabriela asked the other prisoners.

An elderly woman with no teeth nodded. 'Welcome aboard the Málaga express.'

***

So Isabel headed back to Málaga, where everything had begun. None of them knew why they weren't being sent to a prison closer to Alicante but she assumed the Nationalists couldn't physically push anybody else inside them. They travelled in silence, Gabriella and Isabel still kept Maria between them, holding her close as the shock of her sentence sank in.

Isabel couldn't remember when she'd last had anything to drink; her lips were so dry they had started to crack, and she couldn't form enough saliva to wet her dry throat. The train moved slowly forward, and the journey seemed to take forever. When it finally did stop and the women spilled out onto the platform, one of the guards organised for some water to be fetched. He obviously didn't want them dying before they reached the prison. A couple of trucks soon arrived, and by the time they drove up to their new prison, darkness had fallen over the hills. Isabel thought it looked dark and foreboding, and smelled of the damp. They entered in a single line.

The cells were full, but not quite as badly as in Alicante. Isabel had just enough room to sit down if she kept her legs pulled up. Down the length of the long, dimly lit corridor she saw cell upon cell, likely all as full as they one in which they'd put her. Was this what all prisons were like?

At first, the other women in her cell eyed the newcomers with suspicion. They would now have to share any food and water they might get with more mouths, and there was very little given. Their already malnourished bodies turned thinner and many died from the lack of sanitation and unwashed food. Some prisoners got parcels of food from their families, keeping them alive. For prisoners like Isabel, who had nobody, the kindness of her fellow inmates became a lifesaver. Every day they were forced to spend one hour walking around the courtyard. Isabel soon learned that if you didn't follow the rules to the letter you would be thrown into an isolation cell, where they were likely to leave you for a very long time.

This is how Isabel spent her life for the first year. She settled into the routine, made some friends, and even laughed a little in the misery that was the Caserón de la Goleta, Málaga prison. The other women told her about the camps that dotted the countryside, where thousands of Republicans were kept with no sanitation, no food, and almost no water. They died in droves; thousands upon thousands. All those poor souls, who had tried to escape to freedom and failed, had ended up in these hellish camps only to die from starvation, disease or beatings.

Isabel kept close to her prison sisters, Gabriella and Maria. Maria's death sentence could take up to a year to be carried out, and every night she had to prepare herself that it may be her last. The Guardia Civil could come without warning, day or night, and take her to the place the prisoners had come to call The Killing Wall.

Maria developed an anxious facial tick and spent most of her time sitting on her sleeping mat staring at the floor. Isabel knew she expected every moment of every day to be her last. This went on for over two months, when her sentence was suddenly changed to life in prison. Isabel felt sure they did it on purpose: turning someone into a nervous wreck and changing them forever before allowing them to live.

One day, to her surprise, Isabel received a food parcel of her own, with which nobody had interfered. When she opened it up and saw two sugared buns she burst into laughter. Irena had found her and had obviously managed to get herself back to Málaga. Probably in a nicer way than Isabel, she thought, but she was glad her friend was alive and well. After that first parcel, they kept on coming; Irena never came herself, but Isabel became very well-liked as she repaid her friends for their previous kindness in bread and cheese, and an occasional sausage.

To her surprise, Isabel felt something resembling happiness in prison. There were still beatings and there was almost-constant hunger and thirst, and there was horrible illness, but around these women she felt safer than she had in a long time. When it came time for her to leave, Isabel almost asked if she could stay a while longer. She had a tearful goodbye with Gabriela and Maria before she was led out of the prison by a miserable looking guard and walked into the spring sunshine of Málaga.

~ 11 ~

Málaga, Spain
Spring 1942

Isabel started down the gravel road, not quite sure where she was going. It had been six years since she had arrived in Málaga with mamá and Luis at the start of the war. How different it was; how different she was. Prison had made her stronger and she no longer felt lost or alone, as she had for so many years. The captive women had become her family and, through a bond of shared tragedies, they had grown closer than sisters. Now she was out here on her own, but no longer did she want to walk out into the sea and never return.

'Bella!'

She heard Irena's shout from far down the road as she came running towards her. Isabel had hoped she would be there to meet her, but as she hadn't visited the prison thought that maybe Irena was angry with her for leaving.

'You've grown-up.' Irena stopped in front of her, trying to catch her breath after running up the steep road, and gave Isabel a big hug. 'Come, let's get away from the eyes of that vile place.' She took Isabel's hand and they walked through the sunshine towards the city centre. Isabel didn't have the heart to tell her she had planned to go back to La Quida as soon as she was released. How could she not spend a little more time with the woman who had looked out for her all those years, and without any obligation to do so?

They found a bar and sat down to drink some coffee, and Isabel asked what was foremost on her mind. 'How did you find me?'

'With great difficulty. I asked everybody if they'd seen a girl matching your description, and a few days later someone said they'd fished you out of the sea and then you'd been arrested. I didn't believe them at first, but when there were no other clues as to what had happened, I thought maybe they were right. Yet when I went to the police station they said they'd never heard of you. I wasn't sure if the guard was lying, so I went back later and asked again when someone else was at the desk.

'He said yes, you were there, but they wouldn't let me see you. "No visitors until after the trial".' Irena mimicked the guard. 'When I asked when the trial was, he said he didn't know. He also wasn't sure why you'd been arrested, but said I'd find out at the trial, of which nobody knew the time or date. When I went back two days later to find out I was told it was taking place as we spoke.' She lit up a cigarette. 'Honestly, I could have strangled him. I get nervous around places like that anyway and, well, never mind.

When I got to the courthouse you'd just been taken away. It must have taken me over a week to find out where they'd sent you, and for how long, and then I had to save some money to come down here myself. But that was our plan anyway, wasn't it?'

'Thank you for being there for me, Irena,' said Isabel, sipping her coffee. 'I don't know why you've been so kind to me, but if it hadn't been for you I would have given up a lot earlier.'

They sat for a few minutes in silence, looking out over the sea. Isabel then found her voice. 'I can't stay here in Málaga with you. I have to go back to my village. Maybe it's the wrong thing to do, but I have to go. You can come along, get some country air in your lungs,' she said as Irena started to cough.

She'd aged in the two years they'd been apart, and Isabel noticed the lines around her eyes and a couple of grey hairs on her head. But Irena was still a beautiful woman, and her smile was still a little crooked. She was only in her early thirties, yet her life had been tough.

'No, I think I'll stay here. I like Málaga, always have, and I have lots of friends here too. Even one that is rather special, I think. You never know, Bella, maybe I'll get married again. I'll try him out this time, though.' She laughed, and they sat in companionable silence. Isabel wasn't sure if Irena was being totally honest with her, or if she was just trying to ease the pain of Isabel's departure.

After a while Irena broke the silence. 'I can keep an eye on Rosa's grave, too. It feels nice to look after her again, although it's not just her grave. She must be buried with at least twenty bombing victims; there was no time for proper burials. Anyway, I'm trying to keep it nice and if it benefits the others then I guess that's a good thing.'

'I always meant to ask you why she never spoke.'

'She did speak, when she was little. Then a dog—I think it belonged to the owner of the bar down the road from the room we rented—attacked her. They said the dog had just been playing or else it would have killed her. Rosa didn't speak after that. I took her to the doctor once, but they didn't know why she stopped talking and said she was probably just playing it up. What do they know, eh?'

Isabel stayed in Málaga with Irena for a couple of days. They shared a room once again, going out to revisit the places Isabel remembered from her last visit. The war in Europe, and the success of the Nazi's, was front-page news. Isabel didn't know anything about the war that tore through Europe before Irena filled her in. It seemed as though the wrong side was winning everywhere, and the city itself still felt on edge. Irena told her the fascists had killed over four thousand people who had stayed in Málaga or had been captured while trying to escape. This would have been around the time they were hiding from the planes and the shells along the road to Almería. Four thousand people killed, and not even on a battlefield. Isabel could feel the pain and sorrow that clung to the very air of the city, even over six years later.

Irena didn't work while Isabel was there, so she didn't get to meet the man who had entered the same sentence as marriage. She just hoped he was worthy of her.

This she felt even more when the day of her departure arrived and Irena gave her a parcel containing two dresses and some underwear. They weren't new dresses, of course; not many people wore new things, but they were in good condition.

'You have to have something to wear. The prison's left smells on the one you're wearing.'

'I don't know how I can ever repay you, Irena.'

'Come and see me sometime, send me a letter, let me know you're all right. That will be payment enough.' They hugged and said their goodbyes, as Irena didn't want to walk to the bus station.

In one of the dresses Isabel found an envelope of money, just like the last dress she'd given her, and with a smile she put the money in her pocket and felt a little safer.

The dusty old bus was full to the rafters with men, women, and children returning to their villages on their day off or returning to their wealthy employers with special food and other purchases they couldn't get in the countryside. Isabel sat in the back between an older woman and a young man. She tried to see out the dirty windows if Irena had come to wave her off after all, but there was no sign of her. If Isabel wasn't welcome in the village, she would return to Málaga and maybe, unless she had indeed got married by then, they could once again share a room.

The bus started up and Isabel was finally on her way back home to La Quida. The bus only went to the village of Lleida, and from there she'd have to walk. She wasn't quite sure how far, or even the way to go. They had spoken to a man who knew where the village was on her first night in Málaga, and he'd told her to first take this bus and then try and get a lift.

Isabel had decided she'd walk, as she didn't want to spend time in a car with someone she didn't know; someone who might find something strange about her and report her to the authorities. She'd done nothing wrong, but that seemed to be the way things worked. At least that's what the women in the prison had said: Keep away from people and don't talk more than you have to. That way she'd have a better chance of staying out of trouble.

She'd also decided to go straight up to the house, as there she still carried a strong hope she had been wrong about her papá's death. She'd been exhausted and ill at the time. Maybe she'd find him there, waiting for her return.

Isabel closed her eyes and tried to sleep, but it was no use. Once the bus left Málaga it stopped in every village and a never-ending stream of people got on or off. When they got to Lleida it emptied completely, and she asked the driver if he knew the direction of her village.

'It's still a few hours walk from here. You'd do well to stay overnight.'

She looked out the window, not seeing anywhere to stay. The village was tiny, with only a few houses forming its centre, and all their shutters were closed to keep out the evening chill—if indeed anybody lived in them at all. The passengers who had got off the bus had vanished, and only Isabel was left.

'There's a lady, Señora Huildo, just up the road there,' said the driver, pointing towards the road. 'She'll let you stay for a couple of pesetas, and she'll probably give you breakfast as well. Tell her Señor Malla sent you.'

'Thank you.' Isabel stepped off the bus and walked towards Señora Huildo's house. She felt awkward asking for a bed for the night, and even worse having to pay. She'd hoped to be able to buy a few chickens so she would have some food to live on when she got home.

'Two pesetas for a bed, and for three pesetas I'll include an evening meal and breakfast.'

Isabel knew she shouldn't, but she went for the three peseta option. The room was nice, and it was the first time in her life she'd spent a night completely on her own. Of course, she'd slept on her own in the flat in Alicante but had always known Irena was a stone's throw away.

The meal was good, with fired potatoes and onion and garlic; there was even a little bit of meat included in the mix on her plate. It was one of the best meals of Isabel's life, and for dessert she was given a bowl of berries topped with some cream.

She ate alone in the room, knowing the rest of the family sat in the kitchen, probably eating the same food. Isabel was glad they hadn't asked her to join; she wouldn't have been able to relax and enjoy the food as much as she had on her own.

She slept so well that the following morning Isabel was woken by the landlady knocking loudly on the door.

After a breakfast of bread, cheese, and coffee she set off on her long walk home. Even if she didn't eat for two days, Isabel thought she'd still be all right after all that food. How she wished she had enough money to do that again! She walked in the direction the bus driver had pointed, and occasionally, along the road or on the hillside, there would be reminders of the battles that had taken place: a weathered and faded army or union hat, spent bullet belts, and deep scars where shells had exploded.

In the morning sunlight the familiar smells of rosemary bushes and pine trees scented the air. As Isabel walked past, she stopped to pick some, rubbing the rosemary between her fingers. It was the scent of her childhood.

She was getting so excited about being back home, and as she walked along the bend in the road she started to recognise her surroundings. At least she thought she did; it had been five and a half years since she'd been there last. There was the river that flowed between the two mountains, although there may be more places it did so, but what about the rounded top of the mountain in front of her? That was certainly something she recognised.

A little further on she came upon the village, but it looked different. It was definitely the correct one, Isabel had no doubts about that, but the houses had changed. She didn't want to go into the village yet, where they would no doubt wonder where she'd come from and who she was. Maybe her aunt and cousins were still there, but even so she wanted to first go to the house. On her own. She doubted anybody would remember her after all this time, anyway. So, Isabel took the left fork and started walking towards La Quida.

When she passed Señor Chavez's house, she heard someone in the garden and turned to see who it was. By the gate stood a man she only vaguely recognised and thought it might be Antonio. She walked towards him and smiled. 'Don't you recognise me, Antonio?'

She could tell he was thinking about it but shook his head. 'Should I?'

'It's me, Isabel Mosca. I've come back home.'

He looked a little closer and broke into a smile. 'So it is.'

The conversation seemed to end there, as too much had passed to share everything on the doorstep.

'I have to go up to the house. I'll see you later.' Isabel didn't want to ask if papá was there; she wanted to live in hope a little longer. Turning around she started up the overgrown path and wondered why it hadn't been cleared. It didn't bode well for what she'd find.

It almost broke her heart when she saw the destruction of La Quida. The roof had fallen in, and one of the walls had collapsed. The barrels where they had sat in the evening had been covered by a barricade of old wood, stones, and mud, which had since collapsed. It looked as though a battle had been fought in their garden.

She continued towards the house, stopping by her stone. Isabel assumed it was still there because nobody could blow it to pieces, so she sat down and tried to take in the destruction that lay in front of her.

'I'm sorry.' She heard Antonio's voice from behind and turned to see him walking towards her. 'I should have told you down by the gate.'

'It's all right. I don't know why I expected it to still be here when everything else has changed.' For a while they sat together in silence. 'Do you know where my papá is? Is he here?'

The answer took too long to come, and Isabel knew what it would be before he told her.

***

'Here it is,' said Antonio.

They stood by a glen halfway between the village and La Quida. The grass had grown back over where a large hole had been dug; a hole large enough to hold the bodies of eight local men, who had been standing in front waiting for the final bullet, the final push. You could still see its outline, slightly lower and lumpier than the natural ground where the new earth had settled.

'Did you see them do it?' Her voice was barely above a whisper.

'No.' His answer came after a few seconds. 'But most of the village saw them being led away. He's here, Isabel. It might not be any comfort to you, but he died for freedom, and he has some good company. They took my papá, too. Take some comfort that, in the end, he was with his comrades, and they would have been strong together.'

Isabel nodded, but couldn't speak. She'd known he was dead ever since she saw him by her bedside. It didn't matter if it had been a dream or if she'd been awake, she knew he'd come to say goodbye.

They head the sound of a car approaching, and Antonio took her hand and pulled her further along the road to hide behind some trees.

'Why are we hiding, Antonio? What else can they do to us?'

'They can take everything you own, they can put you in prison for the rest of your life, they can shoot you. Best not to tempt them.' He kept his eyes focused on the road until the car had driven past. Isabel saw it was an army truck and guessed he must have recognised the sound.

'Can we go back now?'

Antonio nodded and took her hand, a gesture which she found comforting as they walked slowly back to where both José Mosca and Enrique Chavez had been murdered and buried. She felt as though she'd grieved for her papá already, but the black cloud had never left; it might be there forever. She knew Antonio was correct, that he was buried where they now stood, but a small part of her still wasn't sure. She held onto the smallest glimmer of hope that he had managed to escape, that he was somewhere in the mountains, living on hope and the resurrection of the CNT. She knew she contradicted herself with these thoughts, but nobody had seen them die; hadn't seen the light in his sparkling eyes go out. These were irrational thoughts, she knew, but they were there. She would mourn for him and assume he lay here until she heard differently.

She picked a sprig of rosemary and laid it on the side of the sunken grass. Isabel felt she should say something but knew she would start crying if she spoke out loud so said a silent goodbye instead. Still, the tears came.

Isabel sank to her knees before her papá's grave, sobbing while she tried to talk to him. Antonio put his arms around her shoulders, and she could hear him crying, too. They sat there for a long time, mourning their dead and a Spain that had been lost.

When they finally left, Antonio took her to the house of a neighbour she couldn't remember but whom he said had always been there.

'I would offer for you to stay with me, but it would cause problems. To get work or sell crops we have to go to church, and the priest wouldn't look too kindly on two unmarried people living together.'

'I can stay up at the house. I've slept in worse places.'

'No. I'm putting my foot down. You can't stay there on your own.'

'You're putting your foot down? I got on very well on my own before I came back here, I'll have you know.'

'Well, now that you're back, I feel responsible for you. I'm putting my foot down.'

'I see.' Isabel was secretly happy that he cared, and she didn't really want to live in a house full of ghosts on her own.

Antonio explained to Señora Tarin who she was, and after a little persuasion she agreed to let Isabel stay for the time being, but if there were any problems she'd have to let her go. Señora Tarin seemed very stern as she showed Isabel to a small, cold room at the back of the house. An old mattress lay on top of wooden crates on the mud floor, and she was brought a blanket that had seen better days. Along the other wall was a bed similar to the one she had been allocated, and she wondered who slept there. Isabel longed for the lovely bed and food of the previous night but reminded herself she was now back in her village.

With the family she ate the familiar foods of her childhood, resolving she would pay Señora Tarin when she left in a couple of days. Isabel didn't know what she was going to do, but knew she couldn't stay there, that was for sure.

Twelve of them sat around a wobbly wooden table. A motley crew of in-laws, children, and guests. They ate mostly in silence, but Isabel felt sure that if she hadn't been there the atmosphere would have been quite different. After dinner she was expected to go to her room, so that's what she did. Much later, as she was trying to sleep, she heard someone enter and all her senses became alert.

She whispered into the dark. 'Who's there?' Isabel heard them sit on the bed opposite hers.

'Who are you?' Came the reply. The voice was female.

'I'm staying here for a few days. My name is Isabel.'

There was a deep silence. 'Isabel Mosca? From La Quida, the farm up the road?'

'Yes. Who are you?'

A slow throaty laugh came from the other side of the room. 'It's me. Pilar,' she whispered. 'Bloody hell, I never thought we'd meet again. Well, there you go.'

The room was so dark Isabel couldn't see Pilar, but her presence didn't feel like the girl she used to know.

'Why are you here?' Isabel didn't know why that was the first thing she thought to say, when she should instead say how happy she was Pilar was alive.

'It's best I don't stay in the same place for too long. Is it the same for you?'

Isabel shook her head, although it couldn't be seen in the darkness. 'I just arrived and have nowhere else to go.'

'I saw your house after the battle. That's where I lost my husband, you know. At least he died fighting, not running around trying to evade capture like me and my friends. Where is your mamá and little brother? I remember seeing you all wandering off down the hill what seems like a lifetime ago. You should have stayed here and fought. If people hadn't run away, we might have won.'

So, Pilar was still annoying and full of herself. Isabel didn't want them to start arguing, so she decided to ignore the comment. She lay back down and placed her head on the pillow as comfortably as she could.

'Yes, do what everybody does. Shut your eyes and go to sleep. Let's keep our fingers crossed there's no nightly visitors, as you'd end up arrested too.' Pilar lay down, and Isabel's eyes had adjusted enough to see she was still dressed.

She fired back. 'You have no idea what's happened to me and my family, so don't even think about judging us.'

After, they had no more words and Isabel was glad Pilar hadn't started an argument. When she woke the next morning, after a bad night's sleep, Pilar was gone.

'I met your sister last night,' she said to Antonio as they walked up to La Quida. She wanted to see it again and hoped Antonio would help her rebuild even a small part, so she had somewhere to live.

'You did?'

'Yes. In fact, we ended up sharing a room.'

He sighed. 'She's part of some resistance. I don't know how long they think they can keep it up, but I've already been fined on her behalf and lost the rights to work the land we've had for generations. I dread to think what will happen to Pilar when they do catch her.'

They sat down on Isabel's stone, warm in the Andalucían sunshine.

'I stayed on here to get the crops in and look after the animals when the rest of them went to fight, you know. Someone had to. The way the committee organised it, all available labourers were put to work on everybody's land, the way it was done hundreds of years ago. The crops were distributed to all families in the village according to what they needed, and it would have worked if it had been given a chance. In the autumn, when Pilar came back with her new husband, we found out he was a communist rather than a CNT member and it caused friction in the village. When the fascists were almost within view, he and his men—there were only a handful of them—decided their way of fighting was the only way to save the village and he tried to take control. This resulted in internal fighting rather than concentrating on the enemy, and things turned nasty. When the Nationalists came, we fought them and lost.'

'And that's where he died.'

'Yes, and I can't say I'm sorry for the loss. So many good men and women have died, but I'm sorry to say he wasn't one of the good ones.'

'Is that why Pilar isn't staying with you?'

Antonio stayed silent for a while, looking at the ground. 'She doesn't stay with me because I wasn't at the battle. I'd had a fight with her husband the day before and, well, he came out better than me. He knocked me out and I got sick whenever I tried to move. That's why I'm still here and not in that hole with my papá, or a prisoner in a camp somewhere.' He fell silent for a minute. 'I just couldn't move. I'm no coward Isabel; I would have laid down my life on the battlefield if I had to. I just couldn't move.'

Isabel felt sorry for him, not being able to fight in the one battle he should have to keep the fascists away. She could see Pilar being angry, getting up on the high horse she'd been on the night before. It wasn't fair, Isabel thought. At least she had some family left.

Isabel changed the subject. 'Will you help me rebuild?'

'I would, but I may have to move. To a big city, perhaps.'

She looked at Antonio, surprised. 'Why?'

'I have to find some work. I've been living on what I can forage from the forest, but I can't keep doing that forever. The house also needs repairing.' He looked around, smiling sadly. 'Not as much as this one, but still ... and when winter comes it gets hard to find anything to eat.'

That put paid to Isabel's plans; she couldn't do it alone. 'Don't go to the city, Antonio. This is where we belong, where our families are from. This red earth is ours. If you leave, you'll regret it forever. Can't you get your land back? Pay for it over time?'

'I don't think so.'

'Have they taken papá's land? You could help with that, if it's still ours. Well, I guess it would be Luis's, but he's not here and he wouldn't want it anyway. We can do it together.'

'I don't know if it's in his name or not. Your family had a different lease than the rest of us, that much I know. There is a man in town who can help you find out. He was on the fascists' side but, as much as I dislike him, he's been fair so far.'

'Do you really think he could help?'

'We can ask tomorrow.'

They sat for a while longer in the afternoon sunshine before walking back towards the village, stopping to pay respect when they walked past the glen where their papás lay.

'Isabel, I may as well ask you now, because if you still own the land, you'll think I'm only asking to get hold of it.' He took her hand. 'Will you marry me?'

Isabel looked at Antonio, her mouth open in surprise. 'What?'

'Will you marry me? I know it's only been a couple of days since you came back, but I've thought about you a lot. In fact, I've thought about little else since I saw you walk past my gate on your way up to La Quida. I think it's what they would have wanted.' He looked over to the indented earth.

Isabel felt anger bubble up. 'How dare you say what my papá would have wanted? You have no idea what his thoughts on any subject would have been.' She spun around and started running back to the guest house. Halfway there she stopped to catch her breath.

Why had she reacted like that? Antonio had probably been right, but she wanted papá to be separate from the others in that grave. He deserved better, and so did the others. He might have been murdered together with his comrades, but his last thoughts would have been of his daughter, his wife, and his son, not the Republic or his comrades.

She hadn't been fair to Antonio, but she couldn't marry him; she'd never even considered marriage at all. How could she after everything that had happened.

Once her breathing returned to normal Isabel started walking back to where she'd left Antonio. But the glen was empty, and he was nowhere to be seen. She shouted his name but received no response, so she started walking back up the mountainside towards his house.

How many times had she walked this road? A lot of things from her childhood, from before the war, had faded into the past, but some things she remembered clear as day. This road was one of them, with the rosemary bushes to one side and the drop down to the river on the other. The beauty of the surrounding mountains, standing out against the sky, was sometimes so intense it hurt her eyes.

As she approached Antonio's house, she saw a police vehicle parked outside, and shouting coming from within. Isabel stopped, unsure what to do, but then walked through the gate and towards the door just as a couple of Guardia Civil came out and very nearly knocked her over.

'Papers,' said one, holding out his hand.

Isabel handed him the only paper she had, which she had been given when she was released from prison. He glared at through narrowed eyes.

'A troublemaker. What are you doing here?'

She didn't know what to say. Maybe Antonio would get into trouble for knowing her, and she didn't want to add to his troubles.

'She's here to see me. She's an old friend.' Antonio's voice came from the doorway.

The guard looked back up. 'You can't speak for yourself? Did they cut your tongue out in prison?'

Isabel cringed, knowing Antonio had heard that last remark.

'You took me by surprise, that's all. As he said, I'm here to visit.'

'Put one foot wrong and I'll make sure you go back behind bars. Don't think that because this is the countryside you can get away with crime.' The Guardia Civil turned to his colleague. 'These Rojos are all whores, it's not difficult to see why she's here.' He turned his gaze back to Isabel. 'If she wasn't so dirty, I'd have some myself, but you never know what diseases they carry.'

If he hoped to get a reaction from either of them he was mistaken. Isabel's eyes remained on the ground in front of the guards, willing them to leave. Finally, he threw the piece of paper at her and they walked back to their car. Antonio and Isabel remained standing where they were, Isabel's secret now out in the open air.

She bent down and picked up the identification paper and put it back in her pocket. Is this the way it would be forever? Living in fear and poverty until she died, which would probably be of a broken heart.

When she looked up, Antonio had gone inside. Isabel found him at the old kitchen table, where he sat staring at the dusty air. He didn't look up when she sat in the opposite chair. Neither wanted to break the silence.

She didn't know if he was thinking about the visit, her rejection, or the fact she had been to prison. His dark brown hair hung in waves over his forehead and Isabel felt a wave of affection, even in the middle of this crisis.

Finally, she couldn't bear the silence any longer. 'What did they want?'

'They come by occasionally to see how I am. Make sure everything is fine.' Antonio looked up, his eyes deep as an ocean and full of hurt. 'I'm sorry. I didn't mean to be rude. They come along every now and then to let me know they haven't forgotten about Pilar. Somebody had seen me with a girl her age, and so they thought they'd come by and make sure she wasn't here. I'm sorry you got caught up in the midst of this mess.' He sighed. 'I'm sorry for not standing up for you out there. I would have, once upon a time.'

'I'm glad you didn't. They would just have used it as an excuse to do worse.'

'I would have, if you were mine to defend.'

'I hope you wouldn't. Nobody needs a dead husband because that's what would have happened.'

'But at least they wouldn't be able to take advantage. The things that went on here just after the battle were ...

indescribable.' He glanced at her. 'I'm so glad you weren't here to see it.'

No, but I was somewhere just as bad—or worse. Isabel wanted to tell him everything but found she couldn't yet. 'I don't think they care about that. They do what they want.' She waited for him to ask why she'd been to prison, but instead he got up and fetched a bottle.

'There are no cups,' he said plainly, taking a swig and offering her the bottle. She accepted, and felt the spirit burn her throat as it went down.

Antonio didn't sit back down. 'I'll walk you back to Señora Tarin's.'

They left the house and started down the road when Isabel felt she ought to say something about what had happened earlier.

'I'm sorry I shouted at you and ran away. There are things you don't know about me, things that have happened and ... I can't ever marry anybody.'

He just nodded, keeping his eyes in front of him. 'You could marry me.'

'I can't. Not after everything ... I think I'm broken.'

Antonio turned towards her and took hold of her arms. 'We're all broken, Isabel. Let me look after you. I'll make you a good husband.'

Tears fell down her cheeks because she wanted to say yes, and they kept falling because she knew she first had to tell him what had happened. Only then could she accept his hand.

He put his arms around her, and she felt as though she was wrapped in a cloak of safety. The last time she felt safe had been before the first planes had appeared from the west on the road from Málaga to Almería, and she wanted nothing more than to stay where she was.

'So, will you marry me, Isabel Mosca?'

She stood back and looked into his face. 'There's something I need to tell you first.'

Antonio shook his head. 'No. You don't have to tell me anything.'

'Yes. I do.' She walked over to the hillside and sat down in the dry grass. Then, with a minimum of details, she told him what had happened in Alicante: the abduction, the pregnancy, the prison sentence. She didn't mention the parade; it was something she'd never mention again. She also told him it was unlikely she would be able to have children, as that's what some of the women in the prison had told her after her beating.

He didn't speak one word during her confession of the horrors she'd been through. When she went silent Antonio put his arm around her shoulders. 'Will you marry me now?'

She nodded. 'I will. If you'll have me.'

***

They had to ask permission to marry. It wasn't an easy process, but finally the church and council agreed. Her

Aunt Manda had left the village many years earlier, so Isabel had no family and no money for a big wedding, but some neighbours came to the church and then back to the ruins of La Quida. She'd wanted to celebrate her new life in her childhood home and there, amongst the broken walls and overgrown grass, they drank and ate with their neighbours. The fields now belonged to the old landowner, who had taken them back on the grounds of neglect, but nobody wanted the house. She still wasn't sure José Mosca was dead, and that day, as she did every day for the rest of her life, she made up stories as to why he wasn't there. She'd sent an invitation to Irena but had received been no reply. Maybe it hadn't been delivered, maybe she'd moved, or maybe she'd wanted Isabel to get on with her life without strings to the past.

She still had no idea of how to get in touch with Luis, but she would try once they had settled and organised some kind of livelihood. Antonio and Señor Chavez had been good tenants, even though the landowner had a real dislike for Rojos. He'd agreed that if they could find the money, they could have the fields back. Even though Isabel had given the rest of the pesetas Irena had gifted her they were still short.

Finally, the guests left and Antonio and Isabel were alone at the house. As darkness started to fall she led him to the place where her mamá had buried their belongings before they left. She'd only remembered earlier that day, when one of their guests had fallen over drunk just where they had dug.

'I hope it's still here.'

'What is it you're looking for, wife?'

She smiled up at him and continued to dig. When he saw that she was serious, he joined her.

Isabel's hands hit something hard; it was still there.

It was like opening a treasure chest to times past. There was nothing of monetary value, but they found the old lamp that had lit their kitchen when they had oil and the paperwork for the farm. Antonio said he would find someone who understood legal things, although it probably didn't matter much even if it didn't mention neglect as one of the reasons for repossession. It was good land, and the landowner would probably never part with it again.

They carried the lamp and the other bits and pieces from her childhood down the hill. Antonio's house was now nice and clean, ready for the newlyweds to start their lives.

'Let's have a drink,' said Antonio as they went inside.

When their eyes adjusted, they noticed the figure sitting by the table. 'I guess I should congratulate you two,' said Pilar, standing up. 'I'm sorry I couldn't be there.'

Her voice was full of bitterness, although Isabel thought she also sounded sad.

'We're sorry too, Pilar,' said Antonio, 'but what are you doing here? You made it quite clear the last time I saw you we were no longer family.'

'I just wanted to say how happy I am for you. I'm glad your lives are going forward as if nothing's happened.'

'Don't come here today, of all days, and spread your sour words,' said Antonio, sitting down at the table with the bottle of wine.

Isabel started to feel sorry for her new sister-in-law. She knew how it felt to be the odd one out, the one left behind, the one who couldn't live a normal and happy life. 'Sit down with us for a little while,' she said.

'Thank you. That's very kind. But this is my home too, you know, so don't patronise me.' Pilar sat herself down anyway, taking the bottle from her brother.

'I'm glad they haven't caught you,' he said. 'You should try to get to France. They'll catch you if you stay here, you do know that.'

'What do you care? You're all settled now. I should have had this life, too. I did have it before they killed him.'

'Stop this self-pity now, Pilar. Either you go north to France, like so many others have managed to do, or you go somewhere else. You can't hide in these mountains forever.'

'Maybe she could stay with us and hide here during the day if anyone comes along,' said Isabel. 'Just until she knows what she wants to do.'

'I am right here, you know. Don't talk about me as if I'm not.' Pilar glared at Isabel, but the sting had gone out of her words. 'I have friends, so don't worry about me.' She got up from her chair, grabbing another swig from the bottle and walking towards the door. 'Well, I've said what I came to say.'

'I meant what I said. You're welcome here anytime,' said Isabel. Pilar nodded briefly in return.

Antonio sat quietly at the table during this exchange. He'd not yet forgiven his sister for her behaviour during the war, and she knew it. He would one day, because in the end blood was always thicker than water. The door shut behind Pilar and they sat in silence before Antonio handed the bottle to Isabel. 'To a better future.'

She nodded and took a sip. 'To the future.'

Over the next few weeks they tried to figure out what to do for money. Antonio still talked about going to Málaga to try and find some work, but Isabel still resisted the idea. She didn't want to go back to a big city. She'd have to if she wanted to see Irena again, but then it would only be for a visit. At some point, when they were settled, she still wanted to find Luis and bring him back home. But she worried about him forgetting her. It was now almost four years since she'd seen him last, and she couldn't remember the name of the town where they'd gone. She'd have to go back to Alicante and see Señora Puerta again. Maybe they'd moved back and all would be well. However, Isabel didn't want to go back to Alicante at all if she could help it. The city held black memories, and now that she'd told Antonio some of it she didn't want to ever think about it again.

Marriage agreed with Isabel. She had found a place where she belonged and Antonio did indeed look after her, although they had no money and ate only what they could find or kill in the forest. The landowner finally agreed to take the money they had, and a large percentage of their produce, in return for giving back the land.

The first year passed and, as she suspected, there was no sign of any children. Antonio was all right with it; he was happy having her as his wife and having his lands returned. The amount they had to give the landowner was so large they hardly had any left for themselves, but it was infinitely better than relying on foraging.

They wrote, with the help of some friends, to Señora Puerta in Alicante. When they got no reply, they finally decided they should travel there together. A neighbour would look after their chickens and the two goats they acquired in trades.

The bus was crowded and cold as they set out on an October morning. The rode as far as Málaga, and then from there took another along the coast and up towards Alicante.

It was a long journey, and along the road where two of her family members had died Isabel closed her eyes and tried, to no avail, to sleep. Instead she sat there, eyes shut and mind empty, for hours until they reached the outskirts of Almería. Antonio had never been to the east coast, in fact he'd never before been on a bus, and found he didn't like it.

It was a relief when they stepped off the bus and onto the promenade in Alicante. They stood just opposite the loft where she'd first stayed with Irena, the place where they had watched the desperation of the refugees in the harbour. She had no wish to show Antonio the sights of that awful place and, knowing what had happened there, he too was quite keen to get their business over and done with.

Quickly, they crossed the road and walked along the alleyways to Señora Puerta's. Antonio knocked on the door, and after a few moments it opened.

Isabel broke into a smile. Señora Alva stood in the doorway. If she was back in Alicante it meant Luis was there, too. She was half the size she used to be, and the lines on her face were deeper than Isabel remembered. 'Señora Alva, you're back,' she said, taking the older woman's hand before introducing Antonio. She waited until they had sat down at the kitchen table to ask what she most wanted to know. 'Is everyone all right?'

'Yes, we're all still alive. I assume you've come to collect your brother?'

Isabel hadn't wanted to be so direct, but then she remembered there had never been any pussyfooting around any subject when Señora Alva was around.

'I guess so. We're married now and live in the village where my family belongs. Where Luis belongs. You've been kind enough to look after him for so long I can't ask you to do it any longer.'

'You've never asked me; he wanted to stay.' She sighed. 'It's been a difficult few years for him, and for the rest of us. First, everything that happened here....' She trailed off and

Isabel held her breath, hoping she wouldn't bring up old nightmares. 'And then you stopped coming. Nobody knew how to get in touch with you, and poor Luis thought you'd abandoned him.' Isabel tried to interrupt, but Señora Alva held up her hand. 'No. I know what happened and I don't blame you for not returning, but you should've sent word to your brother. It almost broke my heart to see him search for you. Then I got a letter from someone who said my husband was in a prison in Barcelona and we had to pack up and leave. He died about a year ago, so we came back here.'

'I'm sorry about your husband,' Isabel said. 'Was it the prison that killed him?'

'In a manner of speaking, yes. They sentenced him to death and shot him in the outside courtyard, so everybody could see what to expect. It wasn't just him they shot, of course; it was hundreds. After, there was no point staying in Barcelona. We weren't even allowed to bury the body; my husband is in a mass grave somewhere.'

'I'm sorry,' she said again.

'Luis won't come with you, but if he wants to I won't stop him. Even though he's the only one bringing food into the house, I won't stop him.'

Isabel so hoped Luis would come back home. The house was clean, and she'd arranged a bed with the oil lamp from their house next to it. She'd done everything she could to make it feel like his home, too. She'd take him up to La Quida so he could remember the happy times they'd had there as children, so he could feel the red soil of his ancestry between his fingers. But now she started to doubt he'd want to leave. Maybe Luis felt obliged to Señora Alva for looking after him or thought Pepe couldn't manage without him.

'Where is he now?'

'They're out working. Both him and Pepe. Well, Pepe helps with the easier bits. They'll be home for dinner soon. You're more than welcome to stay and eat with us, but I'm not sure what we have.'

'No, thank you. It's very kind of you to offer, but we've already eaten.' Isabel had just finished the sentence when the front door opened and two boys came in. They had both grown-up. At fifteen Luis looked strong, as if he'd done manual labour all his life—which is what he had done since he first started working down at the harbour by helping the fishermen.

Isabel stood up slowly and smiled before rushing over to hug Luis. He didn't hug her back. 'It's me, Isabel. Your sister.'

'I know who you are,' Luis said, closing the front door and walking into the kitchen, leaving Pepe on his crutches by the door.

'That's no way to talk to your sister. Don't embarrass me,' Señora Alva said, stern. Luis ignored her, and she turned back to Isabel. 'See? I did warn you.'

Isabel was embarrassed, feeling as if they were intruders who had only been invited in out of obligation. Why she thought Luis would be happy to see her she didn't know.

She walked into the kitchen and stood by Antonio. 'You remember Antonio from the village, don't you?' There was no reply. 'We're married and live in a house just a short walk from La Quida. I've made a bed for you. It'll be a good life. You'll be back home again.' She heard the desperation in her voice.

'This is my home, and this is my family.' Luis swept his hand towards Señora Alva and Pepe.

'Please come back with us, Luis. I need you there.'

'I won't leave this house.' He looked at her for a long moment. 'I'm sorry,' he said, and walked up the stairs.

Isabel felt tears well up, but she didn't cry. Antonio took her hand and squeezed. 'Thank you for your time, Señora,' he said rather formally before leading Isabel towards the door.

'Isabel, wait,' Señora Alva said. 'You have to understand how difficult it has been for Luis. He was only a little boy when his world collapsed and everybody he loved left. I'm not saying it could have been avoided, but he's as scarred by the war as the rest of us. Please try to understand. He doesn't hate you, he just doesn't know you any longer.' She walked up to Isabel and took her hand. 'I'm so glad you are settled and happy back where you belong. I really am. I've worried about you every day since I last saw you. I promise, if Luis ever changes his mind, or if he becomes unhappy, I'll make sure he goes to you.'

Isabel nodded and stepped out onto the street. They needed to find somewhere to stay the night and it was getting dark.

***

They had no money to spend on food, so they ate a couple of apples in the dingy little room they'd found a few streets away from the bus stop. Neither of them wanted to walk around the town, so they just sat on the old bed and talked.

The bus left early the following morning and when they got to Málaga, Isabel felt too gloomy to look up her old friend. She'd go back in the summer.

The house welcomed them back with a chilly autumn air. Antonio lit a fire before making his way over to the neighbour's to thank them for looking after the animals. It was quite late in the day and Isabel was trying to find something for dinner. They'd hardly eaten for two days, and she at least wanted Antonio to have something.

That's when she heard a noise from their bedroom upstairs. It sounded as if someone was walking softly across the floorboards. Isabel grabbed a knife and crept to the door, stopping outside to listen. It was silent ... then there it was again.

'Who's there?' Isabel had the knife at the ready in her hand. There was no reply. She was tempted to run to the neighbours and fetch Antonio but instead pushed open the door with her knife held high, shouting like a mad woman.

Nobody was there, but the window was open. Isabel stood in the doorway, trying to see into every nook and cranny before moving across the room to shut it.

On the bed was a small wrapped parcel, and once she'd shut the window, she went over to pick it up. Two sleepy eyes looked up at her, and her first thought was that somebody had left them a puppy. But she very quickly realised it wasn't a puppy - it was a baby.

Isabel hurried back to the kitchen and sat in front of the fire, noticing it was wrapped in Pilar's shirt. She was still sitting with the baby in her arms when Antonio walked in.

'What's that?' He pointed towards the child.

'It's a baby. I found it on our bed.'

He walked up for a closer look. 'The shirt; its Pilar's. You don't think....'

Isabel nodded. 'I do. I think she wants us to look after it, but didn't want to take the chance we'd say no.'

Antonio sat down next to his wife. 'How are we going to explain a brand-new baby? If anybody knew it was Pilar's they would take it and put it in a home. That's what happened with some of the younger children who had Republican parents.'

'I don't know. Will she want it back, do you think?'

He shrugged his shoulders. 'Is it a boy or a girl?'

Isabel looked at him, surprised she hadn't wondered herself. 'I haven't checked.' She unwrapped the baby and declared it was a girl. More than anything Isabel wanted to keep her. She'd felt nothing but relief when they took her own child away, but for this one her heart already ached with love.

'What are we going to do?' She hoped he'd say they could keep the child.

Antonio saw in her eyes what she wanted but didn't want her to be disappointed if they couldn't. 'We'll sleep on it. Tomorrow morning we'll know what to do for the best.' He got up from the chair and put his hand on Isabel's shoulder. 'Don't get too attached, though.'

They made the baby a little bed in an apple box lined with a towel, placing it right next to their bed.

'I hope Pilar's all right, and she wasn't alone when she gave birth,' Isabel said, lying in bed and holding the baby's hand. 'I hope she's not cold.' Isabel sat bolt upright. 'We have to feed her. I haven't fed her.'

'She'll be all right like that 'til the morning.'

'No.' Isabel got out of bed and picked up the baby. 'She'll die if she doesn't get food straight away. Shall I go see if there's any milk in the goats?'

Antonio sat up, tired. It had been a long day and now his wife, at the very sight of a baby, had gone quite mad. 'They will not thank you for waking them up,' he said, but when he saw Isabel was serious, he sighed and got up. 'I'll be back in a few minutes.' He disappeared towards the small barn at the back of the house.

Isabel sat waiting on their bed, the tiny baby in her arms. 'I think you were meant for us, little one. If your mamá agrees, I'll look after you forever. I won't ever let anything bad happen to you. You're so little.'

She knew she shouldn't get so attached, as Pilar might someday want her back and it would break her heart to have to give her away. So Isabel just sat holding her in the dark. When her husband returned, she fed the baby very slowly until, finally, they both fell asleep.

The following morning Antonio walked down to Señora Tarin's to ask if she could let his sister know he was looking for her. One of the villagers overheard and said Pilar had been found in the river. She'd apparently jumped from the edge of the cliff and died instantly. 'At least they didn't catch her. That would have been much worse,' said the villager quietly.

Antonio rushed back to the house. He didn't want the Guardia Civil to burst in on Isabel and the baby, and they were bound to come around and gloat at the death of his sister. It was with relief he noted that the house was quiet and that there were no visitors.

'She's dead,' he said as he walked in, explaining what the man from the village had said about the need to be careful. It left them no option but to call the baby their own; for Isabel it was the right decision.

They decided to tell everybody she'd been pregnant but not realised it until the baby came. It happened, and who was to say different? Isabel felt so terribly sorry for Pilar, who'd thought it better to throw herself off a cliff rather than keep living the way she had. There hadn't been anyone to save her life, as there had been for Isabel. As much as she'd disliked Pilar when they were children, she would always remember her as a girl full of life, on who had always wanted to be her friend.

Apart from going to church Isabel stayed indoors over the next few weeks and then, just in time for Christmas, said their little baby girl was born. Luckily, over the previous months nobody had really seen Isabel as they'd been working every day God sent. They claimed Antonio hadn't mentioned anything as he didn't want to tempt fate.

She was christened Maria Pili Chavez Mosca.

~ 12 ~

**Andalucía, Spain
February 2003**

Isabel sighed contentedly as she sat down on her bed. Apart from the rich golden light that came from her beside lamp the room was dark, and the house was quiet and still. Luis was asleep in Mapi's room upstairs, and Mapi slept on the sofa in the lounge.

She still thought of her daughter as only just grown, even though she was now almost sixty years old. She smiled and hoped she would be all right on the sofa, and silently thanked her for bringing her little brother back to her after all these years. It was the best birthday present she'd ever had. It had been over sixty years since they'd slept in the same house, since the aftermath of the parade and the loss of her innocence, since before her old life had come to an abrupt end.

Sometimes, quite uninvited to do so, her mind travelled back to memories that should never be revisited, and Isabel had to pull herself away in order to get on with life. Now, as she lay down in her safe bed, she tried to weed out the good memories, the ones that should be remembered, from the bad ones—like Irena's sugared buns and how they used to sit smoking at the window in the loft; how Irena has always looked after her.

In the fifties they'd started visiting Málaga every year to meet up with her. Once, while Antonio looked after Mapi, Irena and Isabel had driven, in Irena's car, to the place of her mamá's death. The bush behind which they had left her body looked the same; impossible, maybe, but Isabel thought it must have stopped growing after what had happened.

Even well into the 1960s they were still finding bones of the thousands murdered on that coast road. Every time Isabel read about a new find she wondered if it was someone she'd known: her mamá or brother or that old woman who had travelled in front of them. She couldn't remember where her baby brother was buried, so pretended he was with mamá, warm and well-fed, frozen in time just like the bush.

Isabel was brought back from the past by a loud click from the electrical heater Mapi had bought. It heated the room, but at night, when she slowly lifted her legs into the bed, she found the space under the covers cold. These days, every time she moved, her hip hurt, and she had to tell herself she wasn't the young woman she still felt like on the inside. Isabel would look in the mirror and wonder who the old woman looking back at her was.

She turned around and opened the bedside table drawer, looking for the booklet she'd written for Mapi: the story of her life, and the secret Mapi needed to know. Tomorrow she'd give it to her, hoping that when she read it she would still be her daughter. At the top of the first page Isabel scribbled a final few words. There; done. She closed her eyes.

***

'Luis is in the kitchen and won't stop crying. Thank God there's nothing to drink in the house,' Mapi said to her daughter. 'I'm sorry to leave you, but I have to go with the ambulance.'

'Is she going to be okay?' Mia wiped away her tears with her sleeve.

'I'll call you from the hospital.' Mapi kissed her daughter's head, something she hadn't done since she was a little girl and grabbed her handbag and the overnight bag she'd packed for her mamá. 'Try not to worry.'

'Call me as soon as you know anything.'

Mapi promised, and with a glance at her uncle, who sat at the kitchen table with his head in his hands, left the house and climbed into the back of the ambulance. She sat down next to her unconscious mamá and the paramedic, tall and in control of the situation, closed the doors.

The road seemed bumpier than ever as her mamá's little body jostled with each one, but soon they were on the motorway; sirens blaring they sped towards Málaga.

Only twenty minutes earlier Mapi had knocked on her mamá's bedroom door and, as usual, opened it without waiting for an answer. Only twenty minutes earlier her life had been as it always was. With the shutters closed the only light came from the lamp on the bedside table, throwing a soft, calm glow over her mamá's sleeping face. But even as she'd crossed the room to wake her, she'd known something was wrong.

Now, as they entered the Málaga suburbs, Mapi felt nauseous and held her mamá's hand to stop her own from shaking.

The ambulance came to a stop and the doors opened. Mapi stumbled outside to give the medics room to manoeuvre. As they rushed Isabel into the hospital, Mapi was left alone in a full waiting room. A nurse handed her some forms to complete, then there was nothing to do but wait.

She sat staring at the bright yellow wall, her mind rushing through all the things she should have done, the things she should have said. When her father had died, she should have moved back home to look after her, or insisted she move in with her in Madrid. But she knew her mamá would never have left the village. As long as Mapi had been alive the furthest they'd travelled was to Málaga, where a lady who insisted she call her Irena, not Señora, had let them stay in her flat. That was a long time ago. Irena had died in the late fifties, leaving all her worldly goods to Isabel. Mapi wasn't sure how much it had been, but they'd been able to buy La Quida and the fields they'd worked for generations. It had also allowed them to put Mapi through university. Both her parents had been so proud when she'd graduated and tried to hide their sadness when she left Andalucía for the capital. Maybe that lady, Irena, had been a relative?

Every time the double doors swung open and a doctor or nurse came through, Mapi looked up, hoping to hear how her mamá was. When nobody came, she went to the reception and asked the nurse, or receptionist or whatever she was, behind the counter if she knew what was happening. But she shook her head and told Mapi to sit back down and wait. Someone would let her know as soon as they could.

Mapi went back to the waiting room, choosing a seat with a clearer view of the double doors.

A few minutes later a nurse dressed in a white tunic and trousers arrived. She introduced herself and asked if Mapi could come with her to a more private room. Mapi wanted to ask then and there if her mamá was all right. Instead, she gathered up her coat and bag and followed the nurse through those double doors and down a busy corridor.

The small room was gloomy and smelled of cleaning liquid. A green blind was partly pulled over the window, and on the floor, covering most of the cream linoleum, lay a large multicoloured rag rug. Along one wall stood a low grey sofa, on which they sat down.

'Your mother has had a stroke,' said the nurse. 'It was a bad one, I'm afraid.'

Mapi nodded. 'Is there any chance of recovery?'

'There is always hope, Señora.' The nurse looked up towards the ceiling and touched her cross. 'But it is extremely unlikely. She's comfortable now; she's not in any pain and that is something for which to be grateful.'

'Can I see her?'

'Of course.' The nurse rose and Mapi followed her to another part of the hospital, to a room with four beds. She scanned the faces of the first three patients and concluded her mamá must be in the fourth one. The nurse asked her to wait while she stepped inside the curtains that were pulled around the bed. Moments later the nurse opened the white curtains that had shielded her mamá from the rest of the world. Another nurse, just finished tucking in the bedlinen, nodded and left.

A drip had been inserted into one of Isabel's arms and a machine beeped quietly and regularly on the other side. The white hospital sheets gave her mamá's face a slightly grey colour. She was still alive, so there was still hope she would recover. These days, eighty years was not that old. Mapi almost fell into to the white plastic chair next to the bed.

'You can stay as long as you like,' the nurse said, putting her hand on her shoulder. 'Call if you need me.' With that she left Mapi alone with her mamá.

She wasn't sure how long she'd been sitting there when Mia appeared at the end of the bed. Mapi tore her attention away from watching her mamá breathe. It was almost hypnotic; with every breath she took there was hope.

'How is she?' Mia whispered and sat down in a chair next to Mapi.

'The same. At least it's not worse. Where's Luis?'

'He's outside. He needed a few moments alone before coming in. I think he's having a cigarette.'

'I doubt we'll see him again,' Mapi said, tired. 'He'll have found a bar or gone back to Alicante.' In a way she was pleased because there was enough to cope with and she didn't feel as though she could deal with him too.

'I don't think so,' Mia said. 'Maybe he's stronger than we think.'

'Doesn't matter.' She took Mia's hand. 'I'm glad you're here.'

'Do you think she can hear us?'

'I don't know. Maybe.'

They sat in silence for a little while, then Mia started telling her Yaya about the wedding preparations and how they could arrange to have it at La Quida.

A buzzing sound came from Mapi's handbag and she pulled out her phone. 'I should have turned it off.'

'Just ignore it.'

'It's Gil, from the dig. I should let him know what's happened or he'll just keep on calling. Won't be a moment.'

She got up and walked briskly through several corridors until she found the exit. It was raining, but she found a sheltered area with a few smokers. None of them was her uncle. No surprise.

'It's me,' she said when Gil answered.

'Mapi, hi. I have some news for you. Are you coming down today?'

'No. My mamá is ill and we're at the hospital.' She explained what had happened.

'I'm so sorry. Well, you take care and we'll talk later.'

Mapi couldn't help asking what news he had.

Gil hesitated for a moment before answering. 'We found a body and believe it's your grandfather. One of his toes was crushed, just like his. I was right in telling you now, yeah?'

They found him! It took her a few moments to respond. 'Yes, of course it was. Listen, can I call you back later?'

'Yeah. If you need me to do anything just let me know.'

Mapi hung up. After all these years they finally knew for certain where José Mosca was buried: in the place she used to visit with her mamá. She hoped it wasn't too late to tell her; she'd want to know. *Then again, does it matter right now?* Yes, it did matter. It mattered a lot. She hurried back through the corridors towards her mamá's room.

She could see them from the end of the corridor. Her daughter and her uncle stood outside the room, looking nervously inside. Mapi hurried up to them, her heart in her throat. 'What's happened?'

'I don't know. The machines went off and she started convulsing,' Mia said, her face pale and eyes red from crying.

Two nurses and a doctor stood by her mamá's bed, trying to stop her from dying. The three members of Isabel's family stood staring at the scene in front of them until the doctor shook his head and everything went quiet.

***

'The funeral isn't until Thursday, Mia. You don't have to stay here until then. I know you've got work and a fiancé to go to.'

'No, I'll stay here with you. Anyway, Fernando is coming down for the funeral. You could do with some help, couldn't you?'

Mapi smiled back at her daughter. They hadn't had the easiest relationship when she was growing up, but it seemed to be getting better now she was an adult and Mapi wasn't quite as intense as she had once been. She guessed it was only a matter of time before she became a Yaya herself.

'Mamá never let anyone near her personal things, and I'm rather scared of touching something I shouldn't.' She looked at Mia. 'Stupid, I know.'

'We're all private about some things. I'm sure she wouldn't mind you sorting through her room.' She stood up. 'Someone has to. Come on. Let's start it now.'

Mapi followed Mia into Isabel's bedroom. After her death it felt as though a dark and heavy veil of mourning had settled over the house, as if Isabel hadn't left. Her things were everywhere; her scent and all the little touches that could only ever have been her mamá's were still there. Mapi had dreaded this, dreaded her mamá leaving. There were still so many things she should have told her, and so much more time she should have spent with her. She had no doubt everyone felt like that when someone close to them died, but that didn't stop her from feeling the same.

Mapi wished she'd found out her history; found out more about her grandparents and their lives. She could always ask Luis, but at the moment she didn't want to upset him more. He'd coped very well, and instead of being someone to be looked after, he'd looked after the two of them. His hands almost constantly shook and Mapi expected him to grab a bottle at any given opportunity, but he had stayed sober. He'd been helpful, probably like he had been with Pepe all those years.

'Look at this, mamá.' Mia held out a photograph and Mapi took it. It was an old black and white picture of a man she knew was José Mosca, her grandfather. Isabel had shown her the picture sometimes, so that she would know his face. Apart from that, however, he had very much been her mamá's personal possession. She thought back to the grave site, and her grandfather's body that had been found there, buried deep in the darkness for over sixty years. Had his last thoughts before they killed him been of his family?

Wondering if they were safe? At least he'd been buried with his comrades.

Mia was sorting through the bag Mapi had packed for Isabel when the ambulance arrived. It hadn't been unpacked at the hospital, and from it fell a notebook. Mapi beat her daughter to it.

'You continue doing what you're doing there,' she told her, holding the notebook in her hands. Was this what her mamá had been talking about? The things she'd been too afraid to tell her in person? It was a thick black booklet with gold trim. Mapi could almost see Isabel writing at the table in their farm kitchen, hiding it away as soon as someone came to visit.

'There are tins of food in here,' Mia said, looking at the shelf in the wardrobe behind the clothes. She pulled them all out and let them fall noisily onto the floor. 'That's strange. Why would she keep food in here?'

Mapi shrugged her shoulders. 'We never had a lot of food when I was growing up, and it was a lot worse during the war. Maybe she was collecting it just in case it happened again.'

Mia shook her head like someone who would never understand real hunger. Mapi had known it in her younger years when the crops didn't come out as expected. She'd regularly seen whole families, thin and ill, pass through the village looking for work. On the few occasions they had some food to spare her mamá had sent her out with small parcels to give them, but most of the time they hardly had enough to feed themselves. Her mamá had scoured the forest for food, making Mapi and her father eat most of it. She herself had eaten a little here and there, whatever was left over, and told them both that she'd eaten earlier or wasn't very hungry. No wonder she was such a tiny woman.

Mapi turned her attention back to the notebook.

For Maria Pili, it started.

My darling daughter, I hope I get the courage to tell you what's in here in person, but it's so very difficult to put the pain into words. It's easier to put them down on paper. This is my story, and it is your story too; more than you think. I will start at the beginning, because I need you to understand what we went through so you can understand why we did what we did.

Mapi looked up, tears filling her eyes, at her daughter who was still sorting through tins of food. Her mamá's words from beyond the grave were speaking the words that had never come easily during her life.

'Are you ok?'

'Yes, but I think I'm going to need a coffee to continue with this.'

'I'll make some,' said Mia, putting down a tin of beans she held in her hand.

'No, no. I'll make it. I need to read through this alone before I can do anything else.'

Mapi went to the kitchen and sat down at the table with a cup of strong coffee and some tissues. She continued to read.

You know the house I grew up in. The broken walls are overgrown with ivy and it's a symbol, to me anyway, of the war and how it broke us all with no a chance of ever being mended. It was a happy house when I was little; it was the house our family had lived in for generations, working the land. That red soil is in our blood. When I was born my grandparents lived there, too, but they were old and died before I had a chance to get to know them. My mamá worked very hard helping my papá with the fields, raising me and Luis, and keeping the house looking respectable. Looking back, I can understand why she was always a little harsh with us.

My papá, on the other hand, was the kindest man you could ever meet. I wanted nothing but his constant attention and affection. I think you were like that with your papá, and though it drove me mad from time to time, I think it made me love you more.

I seem to be moving away from what I started to write. Antonio and his papá and sister, Pilar, lived in the farm at the end of the lane; the house where you grew up, and the house where I am now writing this.

I remember when my papá first left to fight the fascists. War had only just started, and I had only moments to say goodbye. My mamá was left with a baby in her tummy, two children, and a farm to run....

.'.. My mamá, Isabel Mosca, walked with the caravan of death from Málaga to Almería. She lost her mamá and newborn baby brother. At thirteen years old she walked along that road, starving and running for cover as shells and bullets exploded all around. It took her almost two weeks to get to Almería.'

Mapi felt the priest move behind her, wanting her to stop talking. Well, he could wait.

'After the war, with the fascists flooding the city, she endured shame and violence as so many Republicans did at the time. She got pregnant, but the baby was taken away and she never saw it again. She endured things as a child none of us could even imagine now. And she wasn't alone.' Her eyes found Luis in the front row, and she nodded in acknowledgement. 'Her father was murdered in a brutal way, and I never had the chance to tell her his body was in fact in the glen we often visited. She never had the chance to grieve him properly.

'Despite all she went through, she was the best mamá a very obstinate and unruly child like me could have hoped for. I hope she is reunited with her parents now, that her papá has got his little Ratoncito back. She will be greatly missed by all of us.'

She moved to one side and the priest eagerly took over. As he spoke, Mapi went to sit between her daughter and Luis. She took their hands and bit her lip to stop herself from falling apart.

When the ceremony was over they followed the coffin to the small village cemetery where Antonio had been waiting for the last ten years. After the casket had been lowered, and the red soil of her blood had been thrown in the grave, Mapi noticed some uncomfortable glances from a few of the villagers but said nothing.

She heard someone walk up behind her on the gravel and turned around to see Mia and her fiancé, Fernando. Her daughter's eyes were red-rimmed and her face pale. 'Poor Yaya. I never knew what she'd been through,' she said.

'I didn't either; not really,' Mapi said.

'It was all in the notebook?'

She nodded. 'And a lot more that I'll tell you about one day.'

'Just make sure you do.'

Fernando had arrived late the previous night and looked tired. 'My family never mentions the war at all. I swear I didn't know about it at all until I met Mia. If I can gather up the courage to ask what my grandparent's story is, then I will. Before it's too late.'

Mapi nodded. 'I've decided to tell the documentary team everything that happened to Isabel Mosca. At the top of the notebook she wrote "Stay courageous", and I'm going to try to do just that.'

They started walking towards the village hall, where there would be coffee and cakes. The days she'd spent with Mia before the funeral had convinced Mapi her daughter was expecting a child, although she hadn't asked her outright. She's simply hinted it would be nice to have grandchildren and asked why she didn't have wine with dinner, but it had got her nowhere. Mia would tell her in her own good time, and Mapi was quite excited. She'd be a better yaya than she ever had been a mamá.

Once they reached the hall Mapi said she'd join them shortly. She walked to the end of the road, then ran up the path towards the old Mosca farmhouse. She ran past the house where she'd grown up, noticing the renovations hadn't moved much further along since the birthday party. When she got to La Quida she could hardly breathe. She bent over and placed her hands on her knees for a few moments before looking up.

There is was: the ruin that had been such a happy place, the ruin that represented the war and the shattered lives it caused. The mud showing around tufts of grass along the hillside was red, the mud that flowed through her veins. Mapi felt a wave of affection for land she'd never felt before.

She sat down to better her breath. The air smelled of early spring, and soon the rosemary bushes which grew everywhere would scent the hillside. She'd always known she had been named after her Yaya Maria and her Aunt Pilar, but she never thought it was because Pilar was her biological mother.

Now Mapi knew why she been given that second name. Another life lost to pain and loneliness. She didn't know who her father was, but Isabel hadn't known either and she was unlikely to ever find out.

She'd wanted to find out about her family history, but never in a million years had Mapi expected this. She had wanted to mention Pilar in her funeral speech, but it was her mamá's moment. She'd make sure that, at some point, Pilar got her moment too.

She looked out over the landscape and realised the bond she now felt had probably always been there but knowing her history had made it come alive. Mapi would tell the documentary team some of what her mamá's notebook contained, and a little of what she'd found out from Luis, then she'd use the rest to write her mamá's story. She'd turn it into a book, and she would write it here, in this house. In La Quida.

For a moment Mapi wondered if she'd lost her mind, but to her it all made sense. She would repair the house and live there; her and Uncle Luis. She might not become a farmer, but this would forever be their family's house. She could sell her flat in Madrid, which would more than cover the restoration and living expenses for a few years. Her mamá would approve, and with a determined smile Mapi turned back towards the village. How she hoped that Encarnita and her family were there. How she would enjoy the look on their sour faces when she talked about Isabel's story.

Walking into the village hall Mapi took her place at the table. Before she sat down, she clinked a spoon to her coffee cup to get everybody's attention. She smiled. 'Thank you, everybody, for coming. My mamá would have appreciated it. I'd also like to say that finding out about my family history and my strong ties to this village has made me realise this is where I belong. I know my mamá would also appreciate the fact that I'm going to stay.'

She noticed the smiles and looks of approval amongst her mamá's friends, and the blank faces of the others. 'I'm also going to write a book about her life. A book about our history. Our lost history.'

FIN

Further reading

If you would like to find out more about the Spanish civil war and its aftermath, I can recommend a few books to get you started.

- Exhuming Loss: Memory, Materiality and Mass Graves of the Spanish Civil War by Layla Renshaw
- The Spanish Civil War: Reaction, Revolution and Revenge by Paul Preston
- The Forging of a Rebel by Arturo Barea
- The Ambulance Man and The Spanish Civil War: Forgotten Stories from Spain by Paul Read
- Prison of Women: Testimonies of War and Resistance in Spain 1939-1975 by Tomas Cuevas (Author) and Mary E Giles (Translator)

Acknowledgements

I want to say a huge thanks to my amazing husband Roger for helping to make my writing dreams come true. I couldn't have done any of this without his support and encouragement.

I would also like to thank Jennifer Dinsmore for her editorial assistance, and finally, I would like to say thank you to my A Team of beta readers, Jade, Mark and Mary. You're awesome.

Thank you

www.ingramcontent.com/pod-product-compliance
Lightning Source LLC
LaVergne TN
LVHW021656060526
838200LV00050B/2376